# TWO FOR THE KILL

## A TANNER NOVEL - BOOK 8

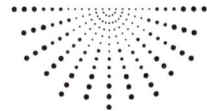

### REMINGTON KANE

INTRODUCTION

## TWO FOR THE KILL – A TANNER NOVEL – BOOK 8
Tanner and Sammy go on a quest for revenge.

## ACKNOWLEDGMENTS

I write for you.

—Remington Kane

# 1
# BONES

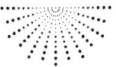

## BROOKLYN, NEW YORK

Tanner fired three silenced shots at the punk playing video games and watched him tumble off the side of the bed and onto the floor.

The man's two companions were in the living room at the end of the hall. They were oblivious to their friend's death, because one of them was asleep with the aid of whiskey, and the other had his eyes closed while wearing headphones.

The man who was asleep died without ever waking, as Tanner jammed a knife past his ribs and into his heart. The eyes stayed closed, although the man shuddered, and seconds later, the body voided its bowels and bladder. The stench reached the man wearing the headphones. He whipped them off and looked about the room.

The man with the knife wound to the heart looked to be asleep, and what little blood seeped from the wound blended in with the maroon shirt he wore.

"Hey Yuri, wake up. Did you shit yourself? How much did you drink?"

"He can't hear you; he's dead."

The words came from behind, and as they were spoken, the man felt the tip of a silencer press against the back of his head. The silencer was hot from its recent use; the punk felt the heat even though it was touching his hair. He was young like the others but wore a good suit.

"What do you want, money?"

"I want to know where Michael Krupin is," Tanner said.

"I don't know where he is. I swear."

"Too bad for you."

"Wait! I don't know where the boss is, but I know where a guy named Bohdan Volkov can be found."

"Why would I care about him?"

"You work for Joe Pullo?"

"I work for myself. Are you saying that Joe Pullo would care about this man, Volkov?"

"Hell yeah, my uncle says Pullo hates him."

"What's your name?"

"I'm Anton."

"You've just made yourself useful, Anton."

Tanner flipped the gun over and smashed it on the side of the punk's head. The kid groaned, went limp, and slid down in his seat.

After binding his wrists and ankles with zip ties, Tanner heaved Anton onto a shoulder and headed out the back door.

There was a car sitting in the driveway with its trunk open, and behind it another body, which was lying near four 5-gallon gas cans. Tanner had killed the man before entering the house, which Pullo had told him was a known residence of several Russian street soldiers.

The dead man had been removing the gas cans from the trunk of the car when Tanner came upon him. They were the same gas cans that had been used to start the fire at the Cabaret Strip Club.

Tanner dropped the unconscious Anton into the trunk, slammed the lid shut, and then climbed behind the wheel. Once he reached Bedford Avenue, he gave Pullo a call.

"Give me some good news, Tanner."

"Krupin is in the wind, but tell me, does the name Bohdan Volkov mean anything to you?"

There was a pause on the line, and then Pullo spoke one word. "Yes."

"I have a kid here who says he knows where you can find him. He's also one of the crew that killed your men and set fire to the club."

"He wants to deal, after trying to burn me to death?"

"Yeah."

"Take him to the clinic; Laurel is there treating one of my guys who burnt his arm. Sophia is there too, and I'll be along once I deal with this fire."

"The club is gone?"

"It's ashes, and it makes me miss Johnny even more."

"I'll keep the kid on ice until you get to the clinic."

"Hey, Tanner."

"Yeah, Joe?"

"We still need to talk… about you and Laurel."

"That's all in the past."

"I love her as much as you do."

"No, Joe, you love her more. It's why she chose you."

"All right, enough hearts and flowers, just tell Laurel that I'll be there as soon as I can."

"Right, but who is this Bohdan Volkov?"

"He killed a friend of mine, Sam Giacconi's son."

"Yeah, I remember hearing about him, but Bohdan Volkov called himself Bobby, Bobby Volks?"

"That's him, and once I find out where he is, he's a dead man."

"That's something I could help you with, unless you'd like to do it yourself?"

"I've got something else in mind. I think it's time Sammy earned his bones."

"The kid? Does he have it in him?"

"That's what I need to find out."

"Right, see you soon."

Tanner ended the call and headed for the clinic, and Laurel.

2

# FRIENDS?

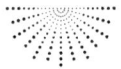

Tanner strapped Anton onto a gurney, then watched as Laurel examined the punk's head wound.

"What did you do to him? The capillaries in his left eye have burst."

"I slammed him on the side of the head with a gun, but he'll wake up soon."

Once Laurel finished with Anton, Tanner reached out and took her hand, the hand with the engagement ring. "That is a very big diamond."

Laurel moved closer. "Say it. Say the words when there's no gun in your face."

Tanner sighed. "I love you, Laurel Ivy."

Laurel grinned. "Do you love me enough to be happy for me?"

"Are you talking about you and Joe?"

"I love him, Tanner. I love you too, but with Joe, I know he'll always be there."

"And I ran away?"

"Yes."

Laurel removed her hand from his and took a step

backwards. "This won't cause trouble between you and Joe, will it?"

Tanner leaned over and kissed her on the cheek. "He's a good man; you couldn't do better."

"How long have you two been friends?"

"Friends?"

"He's your friend and you know it. I think either one of you would risk your life for the other."

"Maybe so, but it wasn't too long ago he tried to kill me."

"He told me about that; he was only following orders."

"He'd have killed me all the same."

Laurel shook her head. "I don't think so. I think he would have wounded you the way you wounded him."

"I was having an off day."

"Liar. Why is it so hard for you to admit your feelings?"

Tanner broke eye contact and looked down at the floor. "I've known Joe for about ten years."

"How did you meet?"

"I handed him a box with a head in it."

Laurel made a pained expression. "I hope you're kidding."

"Actually, Joe and I got to know each other when old Sam Giacconi sent the two of us on a road trip."

"A road trip? Where to?"

"Wilmington, Delaware."

3

GUT FEELING

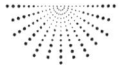

NEW YORK CITY, ELEVEN YEARS EARLIER

INSIDE THE GIACCONI FUNERAL HOME, TANNER ENTERED the office with Joe Pullo and met with Sam Giacconi.

Tanner thought the silver-haired old man was impressive-looking in a well-tailored black suit with a maroon tie. He waited as Giacconi looked him over as well. Tanner was also wearing a black suit, but he had no tie, and the collar of his white shirt was unfastened. There was a holster on his right hip, but only a discerning eye would have noticed the bulge beneath the tailored suit coat.

Sam offered Tanner his hand, and they shook. "Tanner, that was good work you did in finding Vincenzo Rigoletto, and placing his head in a box was a nice touch. I was tempted to mount the damn thing and hang it over my fireplace."

"Now that you know my work, I hope you have more for me."

"I do, and I'm glad Joey was able to find you."

Pullo frowned at Tanner. "He found me. I came out of my place this morning and saw him leaning on my car."

Sam laughed. "You're a pip, Tanner, but if I was you, I wouldn't piss off Joey. My boy here is no one to mess with."

Tanner looked at the two men. "Your boy? Are you related?"

"Joey's as much a son to me as my own, but no, we're not related. Still, that's partly why you're here. I want to hire you to back up Joey on a hit."

Tanner shook his head. "I work alone."

"It's four grand whether you make the kill or not, but the bastard I'm sending you after is too dangerous for one man to handle."

"That depends on the man," Tanner and Pullo said at the same time. Afterwards, they looked at each other in surprise.

Sam laughed. "Yeah, I've got the right two guys. You're both ready to take on anything alone, but I'm telling you, Carlo Conti is no punk."

Pullo straightened in his seat. "Carlo Conti, is that who I'm going after?"

"That's right. Do you remember him?"

"Hell yeah, I was just a kid when he left here, but I remember him. I also remember all the stories about him. If they're true, then yeah, Conti won't be an easy kill."

"Who is this Conti?" Tanner asked, as curiosity peaked his interest. He liked working alone, but he also loved a challenge.

"Conti was an enforcer for the Calvino Family out on Staten Island. We've gotten along well with them ever since Joey here planted old Albertino Calvino and put them in their place. Oh, and Tanner, Joey was only fifteen when he made his bones."

"Some start early," Tanner said. He himself had first killed while only sixteen.

"Anyway," Sam said, "we were at peace, but Carlo Conti didn't like that, so he went on a one-man war against us. Before he finally stopped, he had killed over a dozen of my guys, and when he left, he left with money he'd taken off a civilian. Some guy who was stupid enough to keep lots of cash in his house and then go around blabbing about it."

"How much did Conti get?" Tanner asked.

"Does it matter?" Sam said, and Pullo answered him.

"The more money he had, the farther he could run."

Tanner looked at Pullo and nodded. Pullo was sharp; he liked that.

Sam sighed. "The cops figured he got about thirty grand, but remember, this was back in 1989, so that money could buy more then. And anyway, it doesn't matter, because I know where the bastard is."

"How?" Tanner said.

"One of my guys, a kid named Rossetti; he spotted Conti walking down the street while he was in Delaware on business. He said he was sure it was him, but by the time he turned the car around, Conti was gone."

Joe looked doubtful. "How could Johnny R be sure it was Conti? He had to be only about ten years old when Conti skipped."

"Carlo Conti and Johnny's Uncle Al were tight before Al moved out to Vegas. The kid grew up seeing Conti a lot. He'd know him, and Johnny's a smart one, like you, Joey."

"How old would Conti be now?" Tanner asked.

Sam looked thoughtful as he spoke. "Let's see, it's been about oh, fifteen, sixteen years. Carlo was thirty-something back then, so late forties, early fifties. But if I had to guess, I'd bet he's still the same hard case he always was."

"Why not farm the work out?" Tanner said. "You must know people in Delaware."

Sam leaned forward and locked eyes with Tanner. "This bastard killed my men. We're going to be the ones to put him down."

Pullo looked over at Tanner. "Are you in or out?"

Tanner spoke to Sam. "Just so I'm clear on this. You want me as backup, right?"

"Yeah, Tanner, you watch Joey's back and he calls the shots, but if you get the chance to put that animal Conti down, do it. That civilian he killed, he killed him in bed along with the guy's wife. I want that sonofabitch dead."

The answer was no.

Tanner wasn't backup, he was a Tanner now, and Tanners worked alone. But then he remembered something that Tanner Six often said, and had said to him the day he passed the name on to him.

"Trust your gut, Cody. Your eyes will play tricks on you, your heart will lead you astray, and your mind wants to believe whatever it's told, but your gut, your gut always knows what to do."

Tanner turned his head and stared at Joe Pullo. "When do we leave?"

4

## THE BIG BOYS

FBI Agent Tamir Ivanov made his way past the barricades surrounding the smoldering remains of the Cabaret Strip Club. After Pullo signaled his men to let him pass, Ivanov walked over to stand beside him.

"I hear you had a close call tonight."

"Too close," Pullo said. "And I've already given a statement to the cops."

"Chill, Pullo, I'm not here to hassle you. I just came to see what the damage was and to look at the two stiffs with the rifles. I recognized both of them. They worked for Krupin."

"You wouldn't happen to know where I might find the kid, would you?"

Ivanov laughed. "I don't, and I wouldn't be for sale if I did. But my guess is that Mikey Krupin is in the wind, at least for now."

Pullo looked around. "Where's that partner of yours? She's easy on the eyes."

"That she is, and she's also busy. It seems that someone wasted a Russian crew in Brooklyn, and Agent Moretti is handling that scene. Would you happen to know anything about that, Pullo?"

"Not a thing."

"Uh-huh, that's what I thought you'd say. I bet you also don't know anything about the Italian hoods who are overrunning Krupin's territory as we speak."

"I know that when the boss is away, and his top two lieutenants are dead, that it's a good time to strike."

"Mm-hmm, and it looks like you're about to win this war."

Joe sighed deeply as he watched an ambulance drive away.

"That's right; you lost two men, didn't you?"

"Yeah, Victor and Sal."

"My condolences, and as I said the other day, this war has to end, so win it and end it."

"I don't know what you're talking about."

Ivanov moved to stand in front of Pullo. "Enough of the denial bullshit, Pullo. I'm talking to you as one man to another. End this war. If you have to waste Krupin to do it, then so be it. This shit is getting out of hand."

Pullo smiled. "I'd offer you a drink, but as you can see, we're closed for renovations."

"You're going to rebuild?"

"Damn right, and bigger and better, and this time it will be called Johnny R's."

"For Rossetti? I'd heard you two were friends. You got class, Pullo, thug or not."

"You're not so bad yourself for a Fed, and as far as what you were talking about before, consider it done."

"All right, but don't underestimate Krupin. He's a weasel, and weasels have a way of being tough to kill."

Pullo thought of Tanner.

"I know a great exterminator."

At that moment, Michael Krupin was in a hotel suite in Miami. He had flown down there so that he would have an alibi when the Cabaret Strip Club went up in flames.

When he couldn't get ahold of either Vance or Fedor, he knew there had been trouble, but when the crew who had set the blaze also didn't answer, that was when he started to sweat.

After calling one of his other men and waking him, he waited for the man to report back. When the call came, Krupin felt like crying.

Both Fedor and Vance were dead, while Pullo had survived the fire. Of the four young men who set the blaze, three were dead, and one, Fedor's nephew, Anton, was missing. Pullo's men had also taken over half of his territory, and if he didn't do something soon, he'd have nothing to return to.

Krupin plopped onto the sofa in the suite's living room. As he thought about his options, he heard the words of FBI Agent Tamir Ivanov float through his mind; Ivanov, who had warned him that he'd be eaten alive if he kept playing with the big boys.

"I'm as big as anyone," Krupin said to himself. The words tasted like a lie. Then, he remembered an incident from his childhood.

There was a kid at school during the fifth grade named Bruce who used to pick on Krupin mercilessly. The kid was a foot taller than Krupin and outweighed him by twenty pounds. When young Michael had come home with a black eye and told his father what had happened, the elder Krupin merely shrugged.

"Kick his ass."

"But Dad, Bruce is bigger than me."

"Then find someone bigger than him and pay them to kick his ass, but just make sure that he learns never to touch you again."

Krupin followed the advice. Two days later, Bruce was rushed to the hospital with three broken ribs and a dislocated shoulder. Krupin had paid a friend's older brother fifty dollars to do the deed, and it had been worth every penny. From that day forward, Bruce ran in the opposite direction whenever he saw Krupin coming his way.

"Pullo might be a big boy, but there are bigger."

Michael Krupin grabbed his laptop and booked a flight. He was going to Mexico.

5

# BOBBY VOLKS

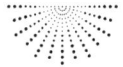

Pullo arrived at the clinic, and after kissing Laurel he eyed Tanner.

"Have you two talked?"

"Yeah, Joe, and I told Laurel that she couldn't do better."

"That's a lie, but she's stuck with me now that she took the ring."

"So, when is the wedding?"

"As soon as the Russians are handled."

"Speaking of that, let's go see if our guest is awake."

They went into the examination room, where Anton was still strapped to a gurney. Tanner slapped his face, which caused his eyes to flutter. Pullo saw that Laurel had followed them into the room, and he asked her to leave.

Laurel stared down at Anton with cold eyes. "He's one of the men who set the fire and killed Victor and Sal, isn't he?"

"Yeah," Tanner said.

"You do what you want with him, but don't make a mess in here."

"Yes ma'am," Tanner said, and after Laurel walked out, he smiled at Pullo. "She's tougher than she looks."

"Tell me about it," Pullo said, and when he stared down at Anton, he saw that the kid was awake.

"My head hurts."

"It could be worse," Pullo said.

"You're Joe Pullo?"

"That's right."

"Who killed my crew?"

"That would be me," Tanner said.

"Bobby Volks, where can I find him?" Pullo asked.

"Who?"

"Bohdan Volkov, he used to call himself Bobby Volks."

"Oh, well hey man, I just know the name Bohdan Volkov because my uncle once mentioned it while he was drunk. He said he helped him to get away when you were looking for him."

"Who's your uncle?"

"Fedor Tarnow."

"He's dead; Vance killed him," Pullo said.

Anton's breathing had been rapid due to fear, but it increased even more as his eyes grew moist.

"I'm gonna kill that damn Rurik."

"You're too late," Tanner said.

"He's dead? Good! And hey, we can make a deal, right? I tell you where to find this Bobby Volks and you let me go?"

Pullo leaned over and locked eyes with Anton. "You tell me, or you die slowly, and I'm talking weeks."

"What the hell, Pullo? Why you being such a prick about it?"

"You nearly killed my fiancée with that fire you set."

Anton tried to shrug, but with the restraints upon him, it looked more like a twitch.

"Shit, it wasn't personal, man. Didn't you ever follow orders that you didn't like?"

Pullo straightened up at those words and looked across the gurney at Tanner, knowing that like himself, Anton's words had made Tanner recall the past.

# 6
# SARCASM IS COSTLY

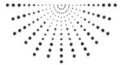

## THE NEW JERSEY TURNPIKE, ELEVEN YEARS EARLIER

After spending an hour in a car with Tanner without either of them saying a word, Pullo decided to break the silence.

"I guess neither one of us is big on small talk, hmm?"

Tanner glanced over at Pullo and smiled. "You've been with Giacconi a long time?"

"I was born into it, and Sam came up with my grandfather."

"I hear you. The family business sort of thing."

"And what about you, you come up in one of the families?"

"I'm not Italian."

"No? Too bad."

"What's our first move when we reach Wilmington?"

"We'll get rooms in a motel that takes cash. The guy

that spotted Conti says the place is a dump, but the owner minds his own business and doesn't ask any questions."

"I assume the motel is close to where this guy spotted Conti?"

"Yeah, Rossetti said that Conti was on foot, so that sounds like he lives in the area. With a little luck, we'll spot him quick and be back in New York by tomorrow night."

Tanner took a piece of paper out of his pocket and studied it. It was a blown-up picture of Carlo Conti's New York State driver's license photo. It showed a man with mean eyes scowling at the camera.

"His license says that he's six-foot-six and two-eighty. I hope you brought a cannon along."

Pullo laughed. "The bigger they are…"

"…the harder they fall," Tanner finished, and then he and Pullo lapsed back into silence.

THE MOTEL IN WILMINGTON TURNED OUT TO BE NOT ONLY a dump, but also a marketplace. Tanner spotted drug dealing and prostitution going on.

"Lovely," Pullo said, as he looked around.

The motel sat off Route 2 and its parking lot had weeds growing through its numerous cracks. The building was U-shaped, with the office on the left side of the U, while sixteen small rooms wrapped around to the other side, two of which had broken windows, while the one across from the office on the other side of the U had a man standing guard.

"He's got a gun under that jacket," Tanner said.

Pullo nodded. "And there's a knife stuck down his right boot."

Tanner took a second look, and this time he spotted the tip of a knife handle. Pullo had good eyes.

"Joe, this is your party, but personally, I wouldn't flash Conti's photo around."

"Because it's his turf and someone might tell him about us and warn him, right?"

"Yeah."

"This isn't my first day on the job, Tanner."

"I can see that, and I think Giacconi wasted money sending me down here."

"He looks out for me, and Conti is a mean bastard. It won't hurt to have you watch my back."

"I'll earn my money, don't worry."

They entered the motel office and could smell marijuana in the air. There was a fat man with thinning hair seated behind the counter. He had his eyes closed tight and looked to be having a fit of some type.

When the small blonde stood up from behind the counter, she looked at Pullo and Tanner with dead eyes.

"You want me to suck these guys off too, Mr. Hellman?"

"What?" the man at the counter said, then he looked over and saw Tanner and Pullo. "Who are you?"

"Customers," Pullo said. "Give us rooms."

The blonde walked out from behind the counter as Hellman zipped up. When she reached Tanner, she gazed up at him. She was on the wrong side of forty and looked even older.

"I'm in Room 4, and it's fifty bucks for the full ride."

"I'll remember that," Tanner said.

"Get on out of here now, Carol," Hellman told the woman. Hellman was fat, going bald, and had beady green eyes that stared out from a face of thick jowls.

Carol opened the door, as across the way three men in

business suits pulled up in a red convertible. One of the men handed the big man guarding the door a wad of money, and he opened the door to the room for them to enter. The room was Number 16.

Tanner looked at Pullo. "What do you suppose is going on over there?"

"I don't know; maybe the girl in that room is even hotter than Carol here."

Carol looked back at Pullo with narrowed eyes. "I understand sarcasm."

"I meant no offense," Pullo said.

"Um-hmm, it's fifty for your friend; for you, seventy-five."

Pullo ignored her and moved closer to the counter. "I want two rooms as far away from everyone else as you can make them."

Hellman's smile was completely without warmth. "Eighty a night each, and that's cash."

Pullo laid money on the counter and received two keys, real keys.

"I guess you haven't upgraded to electronic locks yet, hmm?"

"What are those?"

"Never mind."

"Hey boys, if you want anything I can get it for you, you know, and I'm not talking about Carol. There's better pussy than that here."

Tanner pointed across the lot. "What's going on over there?"

"That's private business, but like I said, I can get anything."

"We'll let you know," Pullo said.

Minutes later, they had opened the doors and were looking in at their rooms.

Tanner made an observation. "I've slept in abandoned buildings that had more class."

"Think of it as an incentive. The sooner we ice Carlo Conti, the sooner we get out of here."

"All right, then let's start looking after we unpack."

"Sounds good to me, Tanner."

"But first we eat."

Pullo grinned. "Are you sure you're not Italian?"

7

## TESTING 1, 2, 3

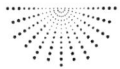

Sophia placed her hands on Sammy's chest to push him away but did so only after the kiss had lasted several seconds.

"Don't do that again; I'm with Tanner."

"Are you telling me that you felt nothing just then?"

They were at the rear of Laurel's clinic, inside her office. The door was open, but Sophia felt as if the walls were closing in on her.

"I like you, Sammy. You know that, but I don't cheat."

"You're cheating yourself. Listen, I don't know Tanner, but if he cared for you, he would have called you while he was away. Instead, all you got was silence."

"I told you, Tanner is different."

Sammy took her in his arms. "You tell me to leave you alone and I'll never bother you again. I swear it."

Sophia stared into Sammy's eyes, and found that she had lost her voice.

When Laurel cleared her throat, Sophia and Sammy looked at the doorway and saw her standing there, along with Tanner and Pullo.

"This is the second time I've found you in this kid's arms, Sophia. Is there something you want to tell me?"

Sammy released her and spoke to Tanner. "We've gotten to know each other while you were gone, Tanner. And I'll tell you right now, I want to be with her."

"And what do you want, Sophia?"

Sophia looked at Tanner, then Sammy, and then back at Tanner.

"I want to go home, and I want you to come with me."

"Let's go," Tanner said.

Sammy let out a great sigh. "Sophia?"

"Goodnight, Sammy."

Tanner told Laurel and Pullo goodbye, and then left with Sophia.

"Sammy," Pullo said softly, and when Sammy met his eyes, he saw the hurt in them. "Let her go, kid. Sophia's made her choice."

"I'm not sure I can do that, Uncle Joe."

"You love her, don't you?" Laurel said.

Sammy didn't answer her but looked at Pullo instead. "I need something to do, or I'll go nuts."

"I've got just the thing," Pullo said.

A SHORT TIME LATER, PULLO AND SAMMY WERE PUSHING Anton ahead of them in a secluded area near the east bank of the Harlem River. Anton's wrists were bound behind his back, and he was begging for his life.

"Aw c'mon, man, I told you everything I know. It wasn't my idea to torch the club; it was Krupin's. He's the boss and I had to do what the boss wanted, ya know?"

Pullo took out a gun and handed it to Sammy. "This is one of the men that tried to fry us. He passed along some info that was useful, but I'll leave it up to you if he should die or not."

Sammy looked down at the gun in his hand. "I've never killed anyone before."

"I know that, Sammy. And if you can't pull the trigger, you can't. Not everyone can, and come what may, kid… you know I'll still love you."

After saying those words, Pullo stepped back a few feet, leaving Sammy alone with Anton.

"Hey! Hey dude, you don't have to shoot me. You let me go and I swear you'll never see my ass——"

Sammy pointed the gun at Anton's chest and pulled the trigger three times. Nothing happened.

Anton laughed. "Oh man, oh you guys were just fucking with me, huh? That's cool. I——"

The sound of five shots filled the air as Pullo fired into Anton's midsection. Anton fell backwards into a patch of weeds, let out a wheezing sigh, and stopped moving.

Sammy spun around and gawked at Pullo. Afterwards, he checked the gun he'd been given and discovered that it held no rounds.

"What the hell?"

"Not here," Pullo said, and moved back toward the car. As they walked, Pullo removed the magazine from the gun he used on Anton, along with its chambered round. With the gun empty, he turned and flung it into the river.

ONCE THEY WERE SAFELY AWAY FROM THE SCENE, PULLO pulled to the curb.

"I didn't want that piece of shit back there to be the man you made your bones on. Still, I had to know if you could pull the trigger."

Sammy studied Pullo's face. "You've got somebody else in mind, don't you?"

"Yeah, and Sammy, it's Bobby Volks."

"The sonofabitch who killed my father?"

"Yeah, it turns out he's been down in Tennessee."

"Tennessee? When do I leave?"

"Soon, but you're not going alone."

"You're coming with me?"

"No."

"Then who am I going with?"

"Tanner."

"Yes, Sophia?"

"I never slept with Sammy."

"I believe you."

"You don't sound like you care one way or the other."

"I don't own you."

They were in Sophia's car with Tanner driving. Tanner had been quiet after leaving the clinic, and Sophia had mistaken it for anger or jealousy. After concluding that she was wrong, she grew angry herself.

"What am I to you, Tanner?"

"I don't know what you mean."

"Pull the damn car over."

Tanner did as she said, and Sophia turned in her seat and stared at him. "Why didn't you call me while you were gone?"

"Most of the time I was gone I didn't know if I'd make it back, and on the trip home, I just figured I'd wait to see you in person."

"You love Laurel?"

Tanner sighed. "Yes, but we're over and we've been over for a long time."

"Do you love me?"

Tanner reached across and stroked her cheek. "I have feelings for you, yes, but Sophia, if you're looking for a husband, I'm not the type."

"I just need to know that I'm more than a piece of ass to you."

Tanner leaned over and kissed her. When they separated, he smiled.

"Of course you're more than a piece of ass; you've got a great rack too."

Sophia punched him in the stomach. "You're such an asshole."

"Can I drive now?"

"Yes, take me home."

They were back in traffic when Sophia asked her next question.

"Exactly what went on with you and Sara Blake?"

"We made peace, and for real this time."

"She's a crazy bitch, but she is good-looking. Just how friendly did you two get?"

"We slept together twice."

"What?"

Tanner grinned. "I'll tell you the whole story, after."

Sophia smiled. "Oh, you think that's going to happen tonight, do you?"

"I live in hope."

"Dream on. And the first thing I'm going to do is take a shower. My hair smells like smoke from that damn fire."

"That was a very close call, wasn't it?"

"If Sammy hadn't known about that tunnel…" Sophia said, and then trailed off as a shiver passed through her.

"I guess that means I owe the kid one for saving you."

"If anything had happened between us, would you have hurt him?"

"I'm not the jealous type."

"That's good to know," Sophia said.

Tanner stared over at her, but Sophia had turned away.

8

# TRAVEL PLANS

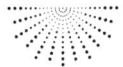

THE FOLLOWING MORNING, SAMMY ARRIVED AT LAUREL'S place and parked across the street, inside the underground parking garage.

As he emerged from the darkness of the garage, he saw that there were men guarding the brick townhouse. They were three of the men who had been at the club the night before, including Big Ralphie. After climbing up the stone steps, Sammy was greeted by all three men with smiles. They thanked him once again for saving their lives during the fire of the night before.

Once inside, Sammy found that Merle and Earl were there. He had only seen the brothers wearing suits and chauffeur caps and was surprised to see them in jeans and T-shirts.

Pullo sat across from them at the kitchen table, while reading the newspaper, and after letting Sammy inside, Laurel had gone upstairs.

Sammy smiled at Merle and Earl. "What's with the long faces, guys?"

"That fire damaged the limo; it was just the paint job and tires, but now we've got nothin' to do."

"I think Uncle Joe has plans for you. Right, Uncle Joe?"

Pullo lowered the newspaper. "What plans?"

"Tennessee, you said you were sending someone with me."

"These two?"

Merle smiled. "I'll go. Earl and me love Tennessee; it's almost like bein' home in Arkansas."

Pullo shook his head. "I had someone else in mind, Sammy."

"Who?"

"Tanner."

"What?"

"You couldn't ask for better backup, but first I have to see if he'll do it."

"I don't need Tanner to hold my hand, Uncle Joe."

The doorbell rang, and Merle and Earl went to answer it. Pullo folded the newspaper up and leaned toward Sammy.

"I believe you can handle yourself, but Bobby Volks is serious business. I'd feel better if you had Tanner backing you up."

"Why him?"

"There's no one better, but like I said, I still have to ask him."

"I don't like it."

"You don't have to," Pullo said.

Tanner walked into the kitchen with Sophia at his side. Sammy took one look at them and excused himself.

"I'll be in the living room."

Tanner watched him go, then turned to look at Pullo. "You said you had something to ask me?"

"Yeah, but do you two want coffee?"

"No thanks, we're going to lunch when we leave here," Sophia said, then she pointed toward the hall. "Is Laurel here?"

"She's upstairs, go on up."

"All right."

After Sophia left, Pullo asked Tanner if he'd back up Sammy.

"If we find Volks, will the kid pull the trigger?"

"Yeah, I gave him a little test last night on Anton and he passed. He also hates Bobby Volks."

"That's right, Volks killed his father."

"Yeah, so it's personal. I know it's not your normal thing, playing backup, but I'm hoping you'll say yes."

"Why not just send me alone? If what I heard about him was true, Volks was a handful. There's always the chance the kid won't make it back."

"He needs this, Tanner. Plus, if he makes his bones on Volks it'll give him a rep, you know?"

Tanner smiled. "You're grooming the kid, aren't you?"

"I won't live forever, and he is Sam's grandson."

"He means a lot to you?"

"Yeah, like blood."

"I'm in. And I won't interfere unless it looks like the kid is in trouble."

"His name is Sammy."

"Right, Sammy. Sammy who wants my girl."

"Is that going to be a problem for you?"

"Yeah, I think it is, but not the way you mean."

"I don't get you?"

"I think Sophia wants him too."

"Oh."

"Yeah."

Upstairs, Sophia lay back across the bed and spoke to Laurel, who was seated at a vanity table and applying red polish to her nails.

"I don't know what to do."

"I thought you chose Tanner?"

"I did, but I can't get Sammy out of my mind."

"I can't tell you what to do, but I will say that Tanner is not likely to ever settle down."

"He said as much last night, so it's not like he's stringing me along. But Sammy, why does he have to be so damn young?"

"That's not a bad thing, is it?"

"Maybe not now, but what happens when I'm fifty and he's still in his thirties?"

Laurel grinned. "I see you've given this some thought."

"What should I do?"

"Follow your heart."

"That's no help."

"I know, but it's what people say."

Sammy wasn't pleased that Tanner had agreed to come along on his quest for vengeance, and Merle and Earl looked even less so.

"Who said you two were going anywhere?" Pullo said.

"We could help," Merle said.

Tanner smirked at the brothers. "You two really want to be around me? That hasn't worked out very well for you in the past, you know?"

"We just wanted to take the trip down so we could

check on our farm in Sawyer's Creek. Arkansas is just across the Mississippi."

"You two own land?" Pullo said.

Earl nodded. "It's only about fifty acres, but it's ours; ours and Laurel Lee's."

"What's ours," Laurel asked, as she and Sophia came downstairs.

"Daddy's farm, we still own it."

"I didn't know that. When I went back to look for you two, the place appeared abandoned, and the house was damaged by a fire."

"Lightning burnt the front porch," Merle said. "But the land is still ours, ours and yours, and with the limo down, this would be a good time to go home and take a look."

"If you two want some time off, take it," Pullo said. "I'll even pay your airfare."

Merle and Earl thanked Pullo, and then asked Laurel if she wanted to come with them.

"I can't just now, but you have a good time back home."

"Okay, that takes care of pleasure," Pullo said. "Now, on to business. Tanner, how soon can you go?"

"We'll leave in two days; I have preparations to make."

"Go where?" Sophia said. "You just came back."

"Joe asked me to lend Sammy a hand."

Sophia stared at Sammy. "Is it dangerous?"

"It won't be for me," Sammy said.

Sophia spoke to Tanner while still staring at Sammy. "I want to talk to Sammy alone."

"Fine, I'll be in the kitchen."

"We'll all be in the kitchen," Pullo said, and gestured for Merle and Earl to follow.

When they were alone, Sophia moved closer to Sammy. "What's going on?"

"I'm going after the man who killed my father."

"The Russian, Bobby Volks?"

"Yeah, did you ever meet him?"

"No, but I know his reputation. Is that why Joe is sending Tanner with you?"

"Yeah, but Sophia, what do you care? I'm sure that no matter what happens Tanner will come back to you in one piece."

"I want you to come back, Sammy. Kill Volks, but you come back here."

"Again, what's it to you? You made your choice last night; you chose Tanner."

"That doesn't mean I don't care what happens to you."

Sammy reached out and pulled Sophia closer.

"Don't do that," she said.

Sammy kissed her, and this time, Sophia kissed him back.

# 9
# A CYNICAL BASTARD

Laurel's townhouse had a small wooden porch at its rear. It looked down on a minuscule patch of grass that the real estate agent had called a backyard.

Although the area was smaller than most rooms, Laurel had beautified it with flowers and an ornate bird feeder. Tanner sat with Pullo on the porch and discussed business.

"What are these preparations you have to make, Tanner?"

"I'm going to get phony IDs for Sammy and me. I also think that once we land, we should separate."

"The IDs are a good idea, but why separate?"

"This town we're going to in Tennessee, Rainberry? We don't know what we'll be walking into. It'll be best if we don't advertise that we're together. And Volks will be less wary of us separately than if we came as a pair."

"Yeah, I see your thinking, and the town only has a population of about two thousand."

"Volks picked a good place to hide, but he should have cut all ties. By staying in contact with that man, Fedor, he screwed himself."

"I appreciate you doing this, and no matter what happens, make sure Sammy stays safe."

"I will, Joe," Tanner said, then he turned and looked through the screen door and into the kitchen. Laurel was there with Merle and Earl, but there was no sign of Sammy and Sophia.

"Something wrong?" Pullo said.

"I'm not sure."

"Sophia and Sammy?"

Tanner shrugged.

"Is that going to be a problem?"

"No. I'll keep the kid safe."

"You're not exactly lucky in love, are you?"

"Is anyone?"

"You're a cynical bastard."

"So I've been told."

SOPHIA BROKE AWAY FROM SAMMY AS HIS HAND MOVED beneath her blouse, then she gazed at him with tears forming in her eyes.

"That shouldn't have happened."

"But it did, and it happened because you wanted it to. Face it, Sophia, you want me as much as I want you."

Sophia held her hands up as if she were signaling someone to stop. "I need time to think. Can you understand that?"

"I understand, will Tanner?"

"I don't know, but I'll talk to him when we leave here."

"Okay, at least I know that I still have a chance."

Sophia hugged herself. "Oh God, I'm so confused."

"I'm not. I want to be with you and no one else for as long as you'll have me. Can Tanner say the same?"

"I doubt it."

"Uh-huh, think about that while I'm gone."

Sophia wiped away a tear. "I doubt I'll think about anything else."

10

## TALK TO ME

MEXICO CITY

MICHAEL KRUPIN ARRIVED AT MEXICO CITY International Airport with two of his men. The airport was massive and extremely busy.

Krupin and his bodyguards weaved their way among the throngs of passengers and made it upstairs to the Hilton Hotel. As planned, they entered the Carlo's Place bar, where they took in the stunning view of the runways and watched flights takeoff and land.

They were soon joined by a group of five men, only one of whom spoke, and the handsome young Mexican said his name was Juan Alvarado.

"My father was intrigued by your offer, Mr. Krupin. He has asked me to escort you to a meeting place."

Alvarado's English was excellent, if accented, and he carried himself like someone who was born to power.

"My men and I are ready when you are," Krupin said.

"Your men will not be coming along, but we've arranged accommodations for them in the hotel."

Krupin swallowed hard. "You want me to come alone?"

"Yes, I'm sure you understand."

Krupin didn't understand, but he also saw no reason why Alvarado or his father would want to harm him. And after all, he needed an ally.

"I'll go with you alone, no problem."

Within minutes, Krupin was climbing into the rear of a limo with Alvarado and two of his thugs, as Alvarado's other two men rode up front. When the blindfold came out, Krupin squirmed.

"Is that necessary?"

"It is, or you can go back to New York City empty-handed."

"All right."

The blindfold went on, the limo roared to life, and Michael Krupin went off to meet his new partner.

Sophia and Sammy walked into the kitchen just as Tanner and Pullo were coming in from the porch. Laurel sensed the tension and asked Merle and Earl to join her in the living room, on the pretense of discussing their trip home to Arkansas.

After Laurel left with her brothers, Tanner looked at Sophia and saw that she wouldn't meet his eyes. He then looked at Sammy and found that he was already staring at him.

"We'll leave the day after tomorrow on an early flight, but meet me at—." Tanner looked at Pullo. "Where will you be working out of now that the club is gone?"

"I own part of a sports bar. I'll be using the back room temporarily."

"Fine, give us the address and I'll meet Sammy there tomorrow night to go over things."

"If we fly down, what will we do for weapons?" Sammy asked.

"I'll handle that," Pullo said. "The Family has got contacts all over the country."

Tanner caught Sophia's eye. "Ready to go, or has there been a change in plans?"

"Yes, I'm ready."

Tanner and Sophia said goodbye to everyone, and after driving only a few blocks, Sophia pointed out a restaurant that she liked. Tanner placed the car in a parking lot that was nearby, and they walked back to the restaurant in silence.

When the food came, it all looked delicious, but Tanner couldn't help but notice that Sophia barely tasted it.

He reached across the table, took her hand, and gave it a gentle squeeze.

"Talk to me."

11

## BE COOL, STAY IN SCHOOL

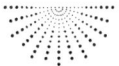

LATER THAT DAY, WHEN PULLO ARRIVED AT THE RUINS OF the Cabaret Strip Club, he spotted two familiar faces.

Carl, the club's lead bartender, stood beside the club's best stripper, Skye, and Pullo was surprised to see that they were holding hands.

"Hello, you two."

When they turned to look at him, Pullo saw that Skye had tears in her eyes.

"I spent a lot of time in that building."

"Don't feel too bad, Skye. I plan to rebuild."

Skye managed a smile. "That's good, Joe, but I'm retiring; I'm getting my real estate license."

Pullo looked at their clasped hands. "Are you two dating?"

"Can you believe it?" Carl said. "She likes me, a woman who looks like this."

"Skye's got good taste, Carl, and so do you. By the way, if you're looking for work, drop by The Americana Sports Bar on Sixth Avenue. Tell a guy named Jonesy that I sent you. They can always use a good bartender."

"Really? The Americana? Great, I'll do that, and thanks."

Pullo left the couple and went to talk to the insurance man who was estimating the damage to the building. Pullo had two bodyguards with him, but they hung back while keeping an eye out.

When he was done getting the bad news about the insurance coverage, Pullo turned to find FBI Agents Tamir Ivanov and Justina Moretti walking toward him.

"Give me some good news; I could use it."

"Too bad," Ivanov said. "We dropped by to let you know that Michael Krupin is in Mexico, and if I had to guess, he's not there for the tequila."

Pullo grimaced. "He's looking to hook up with a cartel."

"That's what we think too," Justina said.

"I know you're winning, but make peace, Pullo; make peace before this city becomes a war zone."

"You said it yourself the first time we met, Ivanov; the war will end when somebody wins."

Justina moved closer to Pullo. "These cartel people play in a whole different league. If they want you gone, they can make it happen. They've been known to wipe out entire families. Put your ego aside and make peace with Krupin, if not for yourself, then do it for those you love."

"I hear you," Pullo said. "But if Krupin is in Mexico it's already too late."

KRUPIN GUESSED THEY HAD BEEN ON THE ROAD FOR WELL over three hours by the time the limo stopped and parked. They were out in the desert somewhere; he was sure of it, because once the engine shut off, the silence was unnerving.

Alvarado removed the blindfold and Krupin blinked against the stark daylight, but as his eyes adjusted, he saw that he was in a courtyard covered in flagstones, with a large fountain at its center. The entire compound was surrounded by a twenty-foot-high wall and there were actual guard towers spaced along it.

Several structures were visible. Nearby was a huge house, a beautiful home that was two stories high, and he could see a barn and a garage as well.

All the buildings were done in the same Pueblo-style architecture, with rounded corners and projecting roof beams. The beams were called vigas, Krupin recalled, a fact remembered from the architectural engineering classes he took in college.

There were times that Krupin wished he had toughed out the trigonometry classes, acquired his degree, and told his father to find another successor. However, it was too late for that now, and the time had come to forge new alliances.

Alvarado's father came out of the home with great difficulty, as the man balanced his thick, hairy body on dual crutches. There were braces on both knees, and one of his arms, although useful, was set crooked, as if the bones of the elbow were malformed.

The crutches gave him the aura of old age, but a closer look and Krupin guessed that the man was likely in his mid-fifties. He wore his black hair long, and there were streaks of white running through it, but the eyes, the dark eyes were young, like the eyes of a baby shark.

"Mr. Mikhail Krupin Jr., you've come a long way to see me. Does that mean you are desperate?"

After hearing the son talk English, the elder Alvarado's fluent use didn't throw Krupin off, and he answered right away.

"Not at all, Mr. Alvarado. I'm simply looking for a partner to help me with a problem."

"You're saying that you can defeat this Joe Pullo on your own?"

"Given time, yes."

"And does the name Tanner mean anything to you?"

"Tanner? What about him?"

"Certain friends of mine have contacts in your city. They tell me that it was Tanner who killed your men."

"I thought he was dead."

"He is very much alive, and if he is as good as his reputation, then I would say you need help."

Krupin sighed wearily. "How much?"

"Fifty percent of all profit."

Krupin's mouth dropped open in shock before he said, "Are you crazy?" and took a step toward Alvarado.

Five guns came out, including the one belonging to Alvarado's son.

Krupin backed up with his hands held in the air. "I meant no disrespect, but really, fifty percent?"

A woman stepped out onto the porch. She was beautiful, and regal, the way only a mature woman can be. Her long flowing black hair billowed about her in the breeze. A man wearing glasses followed behind her. He looked enough like her to be a brother, but he bore none of her grace, and appeared to be older.

"Alonso, why are you conducting business out here in the heat? Bring that man inside and feed him."

The elder Alvarado smiled at the woman, and then spoke to Krupin. "As you can see, my wife is determined to civilize me. Come inside, Krupin. We'll talk over a meal."

Krupin nodded in agreement and thanked Alvarado's wife, a woman who was more than twice his age. As he walked by her, he saw the woman look him over, and in her eyes was the glint of sexual interest.

Yes, he definitely should have become an architect.

12

# ENDINGS AND BEGINNINGS

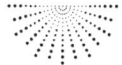

Inside a deli in Midtown Manhattan, FBI Agent Tamir Ivanov was standing at a tall round table, as he watched his partner, Justina Moretti, fend off the attentions of a handsome young man.

Ivanov smiled at the sight. He was in love with Justina and had been ever since he first laid eyes on his young partner. She was a mature-minded woman, even at twenty-seven. However, Ivanov was forty-two, and he felt the age difference to be too much.

He assumed Justina would look upon him as a middle-aged fool if she knew of his longing for her. So, he never said a word about his feelings to her or made a move that could be considered flirtatious. He believed that showing any interest in her would result in rejection, and that he would lose her as a partner as well.

When they first met, Justina was dating a young doctor, but the idiot spent more time on the golf course than with Justina, and she had broken up with him months ago. Why she still didn't have a boyfriend, Ivanov couldn't imagine, but then, perhaps she had a lover that she never mentioned to him.

Justina saw Ivanov's smile as she rejoined him at their table, and she sent him a smile of her own.

"You were watching me, weren't you?"

"Yes, you're my partner and I look out for you."

"Is that the only reason?"

"Joe Pullo said that you were easy on the eyes; I agree with him."

Justina moved closer to Ivanov. She then looked around the busy deli and frowned. "This isn't exactly the right time or place to have this conversation, but I want you to tell me something."

Ivanov was staring into her eyes, while thinking that she never looked more beautiful.

"What is it you want to know?"

"Do you like me, that way, the way a man likes a woman?"

"Justina, I'm much older than… and I… I mean, you're very… um…"

She laughed. "Oh my God, Tamir Ivanov is tongue-tied, that's a first."

Ivanov laughed along with her, and then laid a hand against her cheek. "Of course I like you that way. You're the most beautiful woman I've ever seen, and you're smart to boot."

To Ivanov's shock, Justina leaned in and kissed him. When the kiss ended, Justina smiled.

"I knew you'd be a good kisser, and I have feelings for you too, Tamir. To hell with our age difference."

Ivanov stroked her hair. "I'll be good to you, count on it."

"You'd better. Don't forget, I carry a gun."

Ivanov laughed, then he kissed her again.

After shaking Tim's hand, Tanner was surprised when Madison gave him a hug and kissed him on the cheek. He had called Tim to arrange the phony IDs and discovered that they were in the city.

They met in Central Park, near the Carousel, where the happy sounds of children filled the air to the accompaniment of music.

"Despite all that talk about disowning me, Daddy didn't even have a will. Can you believe that?" Madison said.

Tanner could, and quite easily. He had killed Madison's father, Frank Richards, and even while wounded and lying in a puddle of blood, the man had denied his fate, telling Tanner that he couldn't kill him. A man like that would be too arrogant to consider his own death a reality.

"What's that mean? You get everything?"

"Not all, the corporation was a separate entity and the IRS took a good chunk, but I will inherit money, along with several properties, including the estate in Katonah."

Tim handed him an envelope. "There are your IDs."

Tanner opened the envelope and found two sets of fake IDs, including credit cards and various other things that people carry in their wallets, such as a card for a road service plan.

"How did you get a picture of Sammy Giacconi?"

"Easy, I hacked into the computers for the New York State Department of Motor Vehicles Agency."

"And people say I'm scary. This is good work, Tim. What do I owe you?"

"We've had this discussion before, Tanner. You don't owe me a thing. You not only saved my life, but because of you, I also met Madison."

"All right, but if you ever need me, call that number I gave you."

Madison stared at him, while cocking her head. "Tanner, is something wrong?"

"What do you mean?"

"I don't know; you just look a little sad."

Tanner smiled at her perceptiveness. "It's nothing."

Sammy stepped off the elevator in his apartment building and found Sophia sitting in front of his door.

"Sophia?"

She jumped to her feet and ran a hand through her hair nervously.

"Hi."

"Why are you here? Is something wrong?"

"Tanner and I broke up."

Sammy let out a yell of joy and Sophia giggled.

"I see that makes you happy."

Sammy took her in his arms and kissed her. When their lips parted, he searched her face.

"How bad was it?"

"There was no scene. Tanner isn't stupid, and he could see that I had feelings for you."

Sammy stared into her eyes. "Is this for real?"

Sophia smiled. "I want to be with you, Sammy. You're so goddamn young but I still want to be with you."

Sammy unlocked the door to his apartment and the two of them disappeared inside.

13

## WHAT'S IN A NAME?

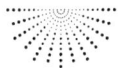

THE AMERICANA SPORTS BAR ON SIXTH AVENUE WAS doing a lively business when Tanner walked in. To his surprise, there was a familiar face among the bartenders.

"Hello, Carl. I see you've found a new job."

"Yeah, Tanner; thanks to Joe. He's waiting for you in the back room there, down that hallway on the left."

"Has that kid Sammy arrived yet?"

"No, I haven't seen him."

"Send him back when you do."

"You got it."

The back room was at the end of a short corridor. When Tanner approached two of Pullo's men, Mike and Bosco, Bosco knocked on the door.

"Tanner is here, boss."

Pullo opened the door and gestured for Tanner to enter. The room was large and appeared to be set up for private parties. There was a bar on the right side of the room, and a giant flat-screen television took up most of the rear wall. The Americana Sports Bar catered to affluent sports fans, and everything had to be first-class.

Pullo sat at the bar and Tanner took a seat beside him but facing the door.

"You own this place?"

"Just five percent of it. I loaned a high school buddy a few grand twenty years ago to buy a neighborhood bar. He turned it into this."

"Impressive."

"Sammy called me this morning."

"So, you know."

"Yeah, and I have to ask again, is it going to be a problem?"

"No, Joe. I'll keep the kid safe. I swear it."

"You want a drink?"

"No."

"I've had news about Krupin. He's in Mexico."

Tanner raised an eyebrow. "That's not good; he could be looking for a partner."

"Yeah, so listen, take care of this Bobby Volks thing and get back here. I'm going to need you, buddy."

"If Krupin comes back with a load of cartel muscle this war will be red hot."

Pullo nodded, and then smiled.

"Why the smile?"

"This trip you're taking with Sammy, it's reminded me of the one we took to Delaware to hunt down Carlo Conti."

"I was thinking that myself."

"We learned a lot about each other on that trip. It's why I trust you to look out for Sammy, and I wouldn't say that about anybody else."

There came a knock on the door. When Pullo opened it, Sammy walked in. He looked over at Tanner, opened his mouth, closed it, and then shook his head in confusion.

"I… have absolutely no idea what to say to you, Tanner."

"Try saying hello, kid, and come take a seat. We've business to discuss."

Sammy walked around the bar and then leaned on it. Tanner removed the phony IDs from the envelope Tim had handed him the day before and separated them.

He would be going under the name of Tom Myers, and his driver's license declared him a citizen of Florida. He slid across the fake ID that he had Tim make for Sammy, then watched as Sammy studied it.

"An Ohio driver's license for… Jack Koff? Seriously, Tanner, Jack Koff?"

Pullo grabbed the license from Sammy, read it, then broke out in laughter.

Tanner shrugged. "I couldn't resist."

## 14
## CURIOUS

WILMINGTON, DELAWARE, ELEVEN YEARS EARLIER

TANNER AND PULLO HAD SEARCHED THE BARS, NIGHTCLUBS, gambling dens, and strip clubs within a five-mile radius of where Carlo Conti had last been spotted, and they came up empty.

By the third day, they were running out of places to look and decided to return to the motel and think things over. Again, there were men at the door to the room being guarded across the way, Room 16, and Tanner admitted to himself that he was curious.

Pullo laughed. "It's probably another Carol."

"I don't know. There's something strange there."

"Hellman said it was private business; maybe it has something to do with drugs, or they're filming a porn movie."

Tanner rubbed a hand across the back of his neck, as

he gazed out the window of Pullo's room at the man guarding the door of Room 16.

"It's still curious."

"No, I'll tell you what's curious, Tanner, Carlo Conti. How could a guy as big as he is stay hidden?"

"Could he know that we're looking for him?"

"I don't see how. Of course, there's always the chance he was just passing through here."

"Maybe we're going about this all wrong. Instead of looking for places where Conti would party, why don't we look for places where he would work? He was an enforcer, right?"

"Yeah, a button man," Pullo said.

"All right, but he's a little old for that now. So what was he before that?"

"I don't know. Let me give Sam a call. I'll use the pay phone by the office."

On the way to the phone, they passed a room where two women were snorting coke. One of them was Carol. When she saw Pullo, she slammed the door in his face.

Tanner chuckled. "I think you lost your chance with Carol, that is, unless you pay her."

"I'd rather screw a goat."

A door opened behind them, and Tanner saw Hellman leave another room.

"Here's the zookeeper of this place."

Hellman was with a teenage boy who was no more than nineteen. The boy was stuffing money in his pocket, and Hellman was fastening his belt.

"It looks like his gate swings both ways," Pullo told Tanner.

When Hellman reached them, he smiled his big phony grin.

Tanner pointed at the room across the way. "How much do you charge for the girls in that room?"

Hellman's smile faltered. "Who told you there were girls in that room?"

"You did, just now," Tanner said.

Hellman smiled the phony smile again. "You're a tricky one, but those girls are very special. I promise you; you've never seen two more beautiful girls. But, I would need someone to vouch for you."

Pullo had picked up the phone to make his call, but he placed it back in the receiver, as curiosity took hold of him as well.

"What do you mean, 'vouch?'"

Hellman smiled again. "It's one of those things where you either know or you don't. But forget about those girls, I can hook you up with whatever you want."

Pullo picked the phone up again. "No thanks."

Hellman looked at Tanner. "What about you, young man?"

"I'll pass."

"Well, if you change your minds, you know where I'll be."

When Pullo finished his call with Sam, he told Tanner what he had learned.

"Carlo Conti started as a leg breaker for a loan shark, but for a while he was also a pimp."

"Maybe he's gone back into his old line of work?"

"Could be, but I don't see a guy like that still hustling girls on street corners."

"No," Tanner said. "But if Conti is in the trade, we'll find him running one of the local whorehouses."

Pullo headed for the car. "We'll grab dinner and plan our next move."

They walked to the car and Tanner opened the door to get in, but then he paused and stared over at the door to Room 16, while feeling a strange sense of unease. After a long moment passed, he climbed into the car and Pullo drove away.

## 15
## EL DIABLO O LA DIABLA?

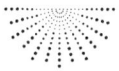

Krupin had locked the door to his guest room, but he woke from a fitful sleep when he heard a key turning in the lock.

He was at Alvarado's desert fortress after the man's wife, Malena, insisted that he stay the night and not travel in the desert after dark.

Krupin had called his men and told them of his change in plans, and that they were to arrange to leave Mexico on the following day.

Getting rid of Bruce, the schoolyard bully, had only cost Krupin fifty dollars, but getting rid of Joe Pullo would cost him fifty percent of all profits.

Krupin had made a deal with the devil, but fifty percent of New York City was better than what he had now. Had he gone back without Alvarado as a partner and the backing of the man's cartel, he likely would have been gunned downed by Joe Pullo. With the cartel backing him, he felt that his fortunes could only rise.

The lithe form slipped into the room as quiet as a shadow and its silhouette read female. It was Alvarado's wife, Malena. Krupin shivered just from the thought of what would happen if he were caught with her.

"You would be tortured," she said, as she slipped out of her robe and slid her naked body beneath the blanket.

"What?"

"You were wondering what would happen if we were caught together, no?"

"Yes."

"You would be tortured, horribly, and your death would not be quick."

"Oh Jesus," Krupin said, then he said it again in a different tone, as Malena eased down along his body and settled her mouth upon him.

He gave in to the pleasure. He knew he had no choice. If he refused her, she would likely take offense and have him killed anyway.

By the time Malena left his room at the first light of day, Krupin knew without doubt that he had made a deal with the devil. However, he was no longer certain if the devil was Alvarado, or the man's wife.

KRUPIN HAD FALLEN BACK TO SLEEP AFTER MALENA departed, as he was satisfied, but tired. He had never been with a woman old enough to be his mother, but found it made little difference, as the woman was as beautiful as many women half her age.

She certainly was more energetic than any woman he'd ever been with. When the alarm at his bedside went off at eight o'clock, he estimated he'd had only slept a total of three hours.

When he left his room, still yawning, he discovered that one of Alvarado's men was positioned outside the door. He wondered if the man had seen Mrs. Alvarado leave his room. If so, it meant one of two things. He was about to be killed, or Malena Alvarado had the men's loyalty, because he was certain that if either Alvarado, father or son, knew that he had slept with Malena, he would soon be a dead man.

When the silent guard escorted him to the dining room, he found the elder Alvarado seated at the head of the table and eating.

When Krupin sat to the left of him, a plate of huevos rancheros was placed before him. The aroma made him realize how hungry he was.

He thought it rude that he was not given a choice of what to eat, but the dish was a favorite of his. He wondered if Alvarado had somehow discovered that fact, or if it was just coincidence.

"Did you sleep well, my friend?"

"Um, yes, very well, thank you."

"That is good. After we have eaten, we will work out some details."

"I thought I would be leaving early?"

"Don't worry. I will have you returned to Mexico City by tonight, and you can fly back the following day."

"I'll have to tell my men about the change in plans, but when will your men be coming to New York to help me take care of Pullo and Tanner?"

"Very soon, and my son, Juan, will be accompanying you on your trip back."

"Really? That's good, but tell me, how many men are you sending?"

"About a dozen."

Krupin's fork stopped while halfway to his mouth.

"That's all? I think you're underestimating Tanner."

Alvarado smiled. "Two of the men I'm sending along

are experts of a sort. They will deal with Tanner, trust me."

"Okay, but if they don't, it could mean the death of me, and your son as well. Tanner is merciless."

"So I've heard, and if I thought I could, I would recruit him."

Krupin opened his mouth to speak, but then noticed the manila folder on the table in front of his plate. Alvarado saw that he had spotted it, and he instructed Krupin to open it. When Krupin did so, he found an artist's rendition of a bearded young man.

"What is this?"

"Does that man look familiar to you?"

"No."

"Look at the drawings beneath the first one, they show him older, with and without the beard."

Krupin looked, but still didn't recognize the man, who in all honesty, appeared unremarkable.

"I've been looking for that man for many years. When I find him, I will give a whole new meaning to the word torture."

"Thank God I'm not him," Krupin said.

When it was time to leave, Malena stood beside her husband and wished Krupin a safe trip. He thanked her for her hospitality and saw just the hint of a smile on her face.

Although annoying, he wasn't surprised when he was blindfolded again, and then Juan Alvarado guided him into the rear of the limo and they headed back to Mexico City.

16

## GOODBYES AND FAREWELLS

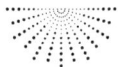

INSIDE LAGUARDIA AIRPORT IN QUEENS, NEW YORK, Laurel gave both her brothers a kiss on the cheek, and then wished them a good flight.

"It's real nice of you to pay for our airfare, Mr. Pullo, and Earl and me will be back in a few days, don't you worry."

"Don't rush, Merle. In fact, why don't you boys move back there?"

Laurel elbowed Pullo in the stomach as she frowned at him. "Don't listen to Joe. You two come back here. You have to walk me down the aisle soon."

Earl smiled. "I can't wait until we're uncles."

Merle and Earl said goodbye, and Laurel looked like a mother sending her kids off to their first day at school. With the boys on their way to Arkansas, she and Pullo then traveled to an adjoining terminal, where Tanner and Sammy were waiting to board their flight to Tennessee.

Pullo took Sammy's face in his hands and stared into his eyes.

"You take care of business."

"Absolutely," Sammy said, and Pullo saw a steely determination in the young man's eyes.

Laurel kissed Tanner on the cheek. "I'm sorry about you and Sophia."

"I have a habit of losing great women."

"You'll find the right one someday, I know you will."

"Maybe there's no such creature."

"Nonsense."

"Have you chosen a wedding date yet?"

"No, but it will be soon, and we'll be keeping it small, but of course, you're invited."

"Maybe I'll catch the bouquet."

Movement alerted Tanner that someone was approaching from the right, and he saw Sophia walking toward them in an emerald dress that matched her eyes. Laurel excused herself to give them privacy.

"Good morning, Sophia."

"Hello, Tanner. I know this is awkward, but I wanted to see Sammy off on his flight."

"I'm sure he'd like that."

Sophia ducked her head and looked up at him. "Try not to hate me, okay?"

"We're friends, Sophia. Nothing changes that. I learned a long time ago to follow my gut, and that's what you did when you broke up with me. You followed your gut."

Sophia smiled. "Gut? Are you calling me fat?"

"Go see Sammy."

Sophia kissed him lightly on the lips. "Thanks, Tanner, and yes, we'll always be friends."

Tanner watched her greet Sammy with a passionate kiss, then he looked over at Laurel with Pullo, and recalled what she said about him finding the right woman someday.

If such a woman existed, he knew she'd have to have a heart as tough as his own.

Moments later, it was time to go. Tanner accompanied Sammy onto the plane and they began the young man's quest for revenge.

17

# RED, WHITE, AND BLACK AND BLUE

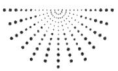

## WILMINGTON, DELAWARE, ELEVEN YEARS EARLIER

Tanner and Pullo had asked around separately and several cabbies had directed them both to a secluded house in the community of Chatham.

The house was a large two-story colonial and they were told that its favors didn't come cheaply. When Pullo checked with Sam, he learned that the brothel was run by a different syndicate than theirs.

"High-priced whores mean heavy muscle, and if they're any good, they would spot the bulge of a weapon," Pullo said.

"Then it looks like we go in empty and acquire weapons if we need them."

Pullo looked sideways at Tanner. "You say that like it's easy."

"It's not impossible, and I've done something like it before."

Pullo studied him. "We don't know each other, Tanner, and if we had to make a move in there to get answers, I'd be trusting in you to hold your own."

"Same here, Pullo, but who knows, maybe we'll spot Carlo Conti the second we walk in, and then there will be no need to ask questions."

"If that's the case, we just follow the bastard and whack him when he gets out of his car."

"Deal," Tanner said. "So, are we doing this or what?"

Pullo stared at Tanner for several more seconds and then nodded. "If you hear me say the word, 'expensive,' it'll mean it's time to take out the security, but don't kill them unless you have to."

"Right, and don't worry, Pullo, I can handle myself."

"Same here."

THE GUY WHO OPENED THE DOOR WAS ABOUT AS BIG AS Tanner and Pullo combined. He was a black man with a shaved head who had one gold tooth showing in his front teeth.

After passing the man's visual inspection, they were ushered inside a huge sunken living room that was decorated entirely in red, while the seven women lounging on the sofas all wore white lingerie. The women were beautiful without exception, and Tanner began wishing he were there for purposes other than to obtain information.

A middle-aged blonde approached them from a doorway on the left. Although she was beautiful enough to entice, she wore a long dress of red instead of the white lingerie.

*The madam,* Tanner thought, and had it confirmed when the woman greeted them with a huge empty smile.

"Look at you two fine, fine young men. You've come here to have a good time, now didn't you?"

"Yes, ma'am," Pullo said enthusiastically, and Tanner watched as he walked over to a love seat where two redheads were seated together. The women's breasts were straining at the white bras they wore, but Tanner saw that Pullo's eyes were trained toward a second bodyguard, who was leaning back against the wall beside the fireplace.

A third bodyguard sat in a chair on the left. Tanner drifted that way, while pretending interest in the beautiful Asian woman who sat at the end of the sofa.

"You boys are new, so let me tell you our prices. Now, for—"

Pullo interrupted the madam, as he lifted a glass ashtray off the coffee table. The thing was heavy, and colored red, like the rest of the room.

"Hey, how much did you pay for this thing? It looks expensive."

Before Pullo had even finished speaking, Tanner had swung his foot around and buried it into the throat of the guard sitting in the chair.

Meanwhile, Pullo had flung the heavy ashtray and hit the guard by the fireplace in the center of his forehead, causing the man to collapse to the floor.

The women screamed and ran for the stairs, but not the madam. She freed a small gun from a holster buried beneath the folds of her dress. As she brought it up to fire at Pullo, Tanner backhanded her and sent her sprawling onto the carpet, then he removed the gun from the holster of the man he kicked.

Pullo had also claimed a gun from the guard he'd hit with the ashtray. He was pointing it at the room's entryway when the giant from the front door appeared holding a sawed-off shotgun.

"Drop it or die!" Pullo said.

The man looked at Pullo, then at Tanner on the opposite side of the room and knew that he'd never get both of them. He tossed the shotgun onto a chair and sneered.

"You gonna regret this shit."

"Sure," Pullo said. "Now help this guy up and go sit over there by your other friend."

The hookers had all run upstairs, but Tanner detected the thump of heavy footsteps coming from above, and they were growing louder. He rushed to the side of the staircase, stripped a tall lamp of its shade, and jammed it between two spindles on the wooden railing.

A fourth guard appeared. He was a large black man like the others. He had been in the upstairs hallway when the trouble began. The man tripped over the lamp as he left the landing and tumbled down the stairs to crash hard onto his right shoulder. The shoulder was clearly dislocated, and he moaned loudly in his distress.

Tanner scooped up the thug's gun, then pocketed the small pistol that the madam had dropped. Afterwards, he helped her to stand and fall onto the sofa. The side of her mouth was puffing up, but she managed to slur out a few words.

"Take the money and leave, pricks."

Pullo unfolded the picture of Carlo Conti and held it up in front of her face while Tanner kept watch over the guards.

"This man, where can we find him?"

The madam squinted at the photo, then she looked up at Pullo. "You're not robbing us?"

Pullo shook the paper. "Where is he?"

The woman sighed, reached her hand into a pocket slowly, and brought out an eyeglass case. When she had her glasses on, she looked at the picture once again, and then frowned at Pullo.

"What the hell are you playing at?"

"What do you mean? You do know where he is, right?"

She did, and when she told them, they knew it was the last place they ever would have looked for him.

18

MIRROR IMAGE

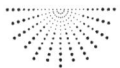

TANNER AND SAMMY LANDED AT TENNESSEE International Airport. After grabbing their bags, the two prepared to split up.

They had barely spoken on the flight, and if not for Pullo, Tanner wouldn't want anything to do with Sammy. However, the kid meant a lot to Pullo, so Tanner would make sure that he came back in one piece. Inside a coffee shop in the terminal, they went over the plan one more time.

"We split up here and arrive in town separately. They only have one hotel, and once we're both booked in, I'll make contact."

"I got it, Tanner, but what if I spot Bobby Volks first?"

"Do nothing. Once we know the situation we'll plan the hit together."

"All right, but I pull the trigger, not you. That bastard killed my father."

"I know, but we can't just rush in. Volks has had plenty of time to make friends down here. We also want to steer clear of the law."

Sammy didn't have a suitcase, but instead, he had packed his things in a backpack. He hefted it onto his back and held out his hand.

"I want to thank you for helping me. I've got to believe that it's the last thing you want to do."

Tanner sighed as he shook Sammy's hand. "Sophia made her choice and I have to live with it. You just make sure you treat her well."

"I will, and I'll see you in Rainberry."

Ten minutes later, Sammy was looking at a yellow SUV and frowning. The vehicle had soccer mom written all over it.

"Is that really the only thing you have here?"

The car rental agent, a young black man in jeans and a white dress shirt, sent Sammy an apologetic smile.

"As I said, sir, the sports car you reserved was in an accident."

Sammy looked across the lot where Tanner was getting a car from another rental agency. They had reserved cars at different agencies so that they wouldn't be tied together, but Sammy was willing to risk it rather than drive a mommy mobile.

"Do you think they'll have one over there?"

"I actually checked before you came in, and no they don't. I'm sorry."

Sammy looked at the SUV, and then an idea came to him. When he asked the clerk about it, the man smiled.

"I'll call and check for you."

An hour later, Sammy was headed for Rainberry while riding a rented Harley.

In Sawyer's Creek, Arkansas, Merle and Earl were gazing at their long-abandoned farm with eyes full of wonder.

Earl lifted an arm and pointed. "It's, it's… it's beautiful."

"Yeah," Merle said. "But how?"

They had parked on the side of the road after spotting the farmhouse. When they left the farm years ago to find their fortune, the land had been full of weeds and the house was a dilapidated mess with a porch blackened from a recent fire.

Laurel had reported seeing the same thing. However, the home was not only in good repair and painted pink and white, but the yard was filled with flowers. Beyond the house, the barn looked renewed as well, while the fields were full of fall crops ready to be harvested, such as cabbages, cauliflower, and beets.

Earl turned in a circle. "Are we in the right place?"

"Of course, look over there. There's that sassafras tree we tied the tire to so that Laurel Lee could have a swing, and across the road is the pond we used to fish in. We're home, Earl."

"Yeah, but it ain't never looked this good."

They returned to the car, and when they reached the driveway, they saw a new mailbox that had the name COLE written on it. They shrugged at each other and drove on.

After parking at the side of the house near an old motor home, they went up the front steps, where there were identical porch swings hanging on either side of the wide front door. Stained glass was set in the new oak door and it sparkled and reflected light in dazzling colors.

"What the hell is goin' on?" Merle said, and Earl just shook his head in confusion.

Although he felt foolish doing it, Merle reached out and rang the bell of his own home. No one answered, and after trying the doorknob and finding that the door was unlocked, he and Earl entered.

The interior matched the outside of the home, as the furniture in the living room looked well cared for and polished, while the rug was new, and logs laid beside the fireplace in a neat stack. There was also an upright piano in one corner, with a guitar case leaned up against it.

A line of pictures sat on the mantle above the fireplace. Merle was about to walk over and look at them when he felt the barrel of a shotgun dig into his ribs.

"Around here, we kill trespassers."

Merle turned his head slowly, and when he saw the face of the woman holding the shotgun, he smiled.

"Wow, you're pretty."

The woman blushed, and when Merle looked over at his brother, he saw another woman, but where the first one was blonde, her sister's hair was redder, or a strawberry color. Other than that, the two women could pass for twins, and looked to be about thirty-five.

Merle's assessment of "pretty" was accurate enough, and although the sisters would never win a beauty pageant, they were cute, and stood only five-foot-two.

The strawberry blonde was holding a revolver on Earl, but Earl was gazing at her as if she were offering him flowers.

"Who are you ladies?" Merle said.

"You're in our house, that's who we are," said the woman holding the revolver.

"Un-uh," Merle said. "This is our house. We're Merle and Earl Carter. I'm Merle and that there is Earl."

The sisters looked at each other, then the one with the shotgun spoke to Merle.

"You used to live here, didn't you?"

"We grew up here."

"I know that. There's markin's on the pantry door in the kitchen showin' how tall you were at different ages. We always figured you two for midgets since the markin's stopped at about four feet."

Merle's expression saddened. "Our mama did that, and that's how tall we were when she died."

The woman with the revolver lowered it. "Oh, that's so sad."

"Sad or not," said her sister, "it don't give them the right to just walk in here."

"What's your name?" Merle said.

"I'm Hanna and she's Savannah; we're the Cole sisters."

"Well, Miss Hanna, this here is Earl and me's home, and you two are the ones trespassin'."

Hanna squinted her eyes. "Savannah, call the cops."

# 19
# YIPPEE-KI-YAY

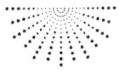

Tanner parked at a rest stop on I-40 West.

After tucking an envelope full of cash under the passenger seat, he left his rented car unlocked. Before walking away from the vehicle with the keys in hand, he tied a yellow bandana around the side-view mirror.

He went inside to use the bathroom, then strolled about the interior of the rest stop, casually observing the other people before heading back out to the car fifteen minutes later.

The bandana was gone along with the envelope full of cash, while the car was locked, and on the floor in front of the passenger seat was a plain cardboard box.

Tanner pulled back onto the highway, took the first exit, and drove randomly. When he was certain he wasn't being followed, he parked in the back corner of a Walmart parking lot.

After getting out of the car, he got down on the ground to check the vehicle's undercarriage for a tracking device. He found none, checked the trunk as well as the car's interior, and then finally opened the box.

Inside, were two Glock 19s, and as he had asked, they had been modified with laser-enhanced guide rods. The guns had spare magazines, cleaning kits, and there were two flip-top 100 round ammo boxes of 9mm bullets.

Besides the guns and ammo, there were two knives with sheaths. Tanner slid one of the knives down into his boot. Feeling better now that he was armed, he started the car and headed back to the highway.

Rainberry, Tennessee, wasn't the quiet little town that Tanner thought it would be. By the time he reached the town's center, he saw a drug deal go down on a street corner and two men engaged in a fistfight.

Other than that, the place did look quiet, even picturesque. Maybe the two scenes he'd witnessed were anomalies.

Tanner was in a bad mood, as his mind had been preoccupied by thoughts of Laurel and Sophia, and he didn't like it. He might not be the one pulling the trigger, but he was still on a hit, still out to fulfill a contract, and he needed to keep his mind on the task.

Laurel was better off with Pullo, and if Sophia wanted Sammy, then she could have him. There was no shortage of women in the world and his lifestyle was hardly conducive to wedded life.

He stepped out of the car in front of the Rainberry Hotel, but then spotted the pub across the way. Checking into the hotel could wait. He was hungry, and a beer would hit the spot as well.

The pub was called The Roundup, and the theme was western, with the walls decorated with movie posters of films about the Old West.

There was a bar on the right past a few scattered tables, while on the left side was a line of booths. Tanner took the stool farthest from the door and gazed up at the menu above the bar.

The bartender, a tall pleasant man with a red face, poured his beer and took his order, but when the food came, it was delivered by a woman who caught Tanner's eye.

The woman looked to be in her mid-thirties, with straight hair that hung past her shoulders. She was beautiful, black, and her huge brown eyes flowed over Tanner, as his own eyes devoured her as well.

When she smiled, she displayed straight white teeth, and when she spoke, it was in a lyrical southern accent.

"You're not from around here, because I would remember you."

"And I'll never forget you," Tanner said, and saw her smile widen.

"I'm Susan Holmes; welcome to my place."

"I'm Tom Myers," Tanner said, then he pointed at the posters adorning the walls. "Are those yours?"

"They sure are, and I'll give you a free meal if you can name the years they were released."

Tanner not only told her what year each film came out, but he also gave a brief synopsis of all the movies. When he was done, he saw Susan grinning at him.

"You're too young to know that."

"So are you."

"My granddaddy was a western movie stuntman in Hollywood before he met my grandma and moved here. He was in about half of those pictures. And before you ask, yes, he was white."

"I wasn't going to ask."

"Okay, but how do you know so much about old westerns?"

Tanner looked lost in thought for a moment before answering. "My father loved those movies. I used to watch them with him on Saturday afternoons when I was a kid."

Susan took the stool beside him. "You say that wistfully. Is your daddy dead?"

"Yeah."

"Sorry, I didn't mean to stir up bad memories."

"Actually, you did the opposite; I haven't thought about those Saturday afternoons for years."

"Are you staying in town, Tom, or passing through?"

"I'm staying for a day or two."

"At the Rainberry across the street?"

"Yeah, but I haven't checked in yet."

"Don't. I also own a Bed & Breakfast. It's empty right now because it's the off-season, but I'm the best cook in town."

"Sounds good to me."

"Don't you want to know how much I charge?"

"No, I just want to spend more time with you."

Susan laughed and stood up. "I'll go get you another beer."

Tanner watched her go, liking the view, and his bad mood vanished like smoke in a breeze.

## 20

# WELCOME TO RAINBERRY

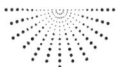

SAMMY HAD BEEN HAVING SO MUCH FUN ON HIS RENTED Harley that he hadn't realized he'd been speeding, that is, until he spotted the flashing lights in the mirror, which were soon joined by a siren.

He pulled over while cursing his stupidity. He was in Tennessee under a phony name for the purpose of committing murder, and before he even reached his destination he was coming to the attention of the police.

After removing his helmet, he took out his fake license and cursed Tanner once again for choosing the name, Jack Koff. To his shock, the cop opened her door and leveled her weapon at him.

"Get down on the ground, now!"

A dozen different thoughts passed through Sammy's mind, including a scenario that involved Tanner setting him up. However, he pushed his paranoia aside and did as the cop said, to lie flat on the roadway with his arms held out in front of him.

When a tractor-trailer passed by coming the other way, it blew up a storm of grit that blinded Sammy. The cop was on him while he was still blinking his eyes free of the debris, and before he realized it, she had cuffed his hands behind his back.

"What's going on? All I did was speed a little."

"Be quiet," the cop said, then she went through his saddlebags and backpack.

Sammy studied her while she did so and saw that she was a young blonde woman with a no-nonsense expression. The seriousness of her demeanor didn't take away from her beauty, nor did her mannish uniform hide her curves.

Sammy had dropped the driver's license. When the woman read it, she seemed to relax a bit.

"Mr. …Koff? What is the purpose for your visit to Rainberry?"

"I'm here to meet a friend, why?"

"Are you a member of the Calabrese Motorcycle Club?"

"No, and the bike is rented."

The cop studied the bike, and when she spotted the sticker denoting the name of the rental company in Nashville, she looked abashed. The handcuffs came off quicker than they went on, and when she handed Sammy back his license, he saw that her cheeks were red.

"I apologize for the treatment, sir, but we've a group of bikers raising a ruckus around here lately."

"What kind of ruckus?"

"We suspect them of being involved with drug running, but never mind that, you just get on your way, and I apologize again for the cuffs."

Sammy blinked. "Wow, you're a lot nicer than most cops. Where I come from, you'd never hear a cop apologize for anything."

The cop shrugged. "I was wrong."

Sammy saw that her name tag read Sawyer, but he asked her first name.

"It's Amy… and are you hitting on me?"

"I was just curious. I have a girlfriend."

"Lucky girl. Now you slow down, you hear?"

"I hear, and you be careful with those bikers."

Sammy watched Amy climb into her patrol car and then rode along behind her on his bike. One of the things Pullo had told him before he left was that Bobby Volks always rode a motorcycle, even during the winter.

Maybe Volks was part of the Calabrese Motorcycle Club. If so, they would soon be short one member.

21

# DUMB AND DUMBER MEET BLONDE AND BLONDER

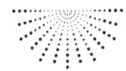

"Phony? What do you mean that it's phony?" Hanna Cole said.

Chief of Police Wilbur Meadows looked as if he swallowed something bad, and after burping, the lanky, gray-haired gentleman settled behind his desk. He then asked Hanna and Savannah to take seats in front of it, as Merle and Earl stood to their right.

"The state records department shows that these two here are the rightful owners of that property. They may not have been living there, but they kept up the taxes, so it's theirs."

"We paid taxes too." Hanna said. "We prepaid ahead for two years. Our real estate lady handled it."

Chief Meadows leaned forward. "Who sold you that property and when?"

"She was a nice woman. Her name was Mrs. Loyola Smith. We ran into her when we were lookin' for a place to buy and she pointed us at that land."

"Oh Lordy, I was afraid of that. Mrs. Loyola Smith was a con woman named Lois Simmons. She's dead now, killed by one of her partners. She used that real estate woman act to identify houses for her partners to rob. You two are the first I've heard of that bought a house from her."

Savannah wiped at her eyes. "Our deed is really a fake?"

"Yes ma'am, I'm afraid so."

Hanna sniffled, and wiped at her own tears. "But we paid for it and then we put a lot of money into that place too. I've got a little garden in the back, the crops are doin' nicely—do we at least get to keep the crops?"

"I'm no lawyer, but my guess is that it would be up to the two Mr. Carters here."

Hanna gazed over at Merle and Earl with eyes full of sorrow. "We're sorry; we didn't know the property was really yours."

"You two hungry?" Merle asked.

"What?" Hanna said.

"Food. Earl and me are starvin' and there's a McDonald's right down the road. Why don't we go there and talk things over?"

"You ain't mad at us?" Hanna asked.

Merle let out a sigh. "Me and Earl been tricked a time or two, so we know how it feels. Hell, we'll think of somethin', but let's go eat."

Hanna looked at her sister and saw that Savannah was smiling at Earl.

"All right, we'll go eat, but we pay," Hanna said.

They told the chief goodbye and headed for the door. As they were walking out, a female deputy entered the chief's office. Once the foursome had departed, the deputy asked a question.

"Were those two sets of twins that just left here?"

The chief laughed. "No, but they're darn close, aren't they?"

"I'll say."

∼

AFTER CALLING LAUREL AND GETTING HER OPINION, MERLE and Earl offered the Cole sisters a deal while they ate.

"Our sister, Laurel Lee, she agreed with us that it wouldn't be right to kick you out of the house. So why don't you two stay there while me and Earl live in that old motor home I saw?"

"That's fine for now, Merle, but what about the future and all the money we put in that house?" Hanna said.

"You could rent it from us cheap."

"I don't wanna rent, it's why I bought a house," Hanna said.

Savannah smiled at Earl. "You don't talk much, do you?"

"Sometimes," Earl said, and then he smiled back at her.

After swallowing the last of her French fries, Hanna asked Merle a question.

"Could we buy the house from you, you know, real cheap? After all, we put all the work and money into it."

"I don't wanna sell. Me and Earl were born there, and so was our daddy."

"I don't know what to do," Hanna said.

"I do," said Savannah. "I wanna go to the movies."

"How's that going to help?" her sister asked.

"It'll take our minds off of things. Do you wanna go, Earl?"

Earl nodded as he grinned stupidly at Savannah.

"All right, then let's go. The picture should be starting soon."

"We'll follow you," Merle said.

ONCE THEY WERE IN THEIR CAR ALONE, SAVANNAH GRABBED her sister's arm.

"Earl is mine, do you hear me?"

"You can have him; Merle's cuter."

"Un-uh."

"Um-hmm."

"Un-uh."

"Um-hmm."

"Un-uh."

"Um-hmm."

INSIDE THE BOYS' RENTED CAR, A SIMILAR EXCHANGE WAS taking place.

"Savannah is cute," Earl said.

"You can keep her; I like the blonde one."

"They's both blonde, Merle."

"Yeah, but Hanna's hotter."

"Un-uh."

"Um-hmm."

"Un-uh."

"Um-hmm."

"Un-uh."

"Um-hmm."

And so it went.

22

# DIRTY BOY

Susan Holmes' bed & breakfast was quaint and sat near a small stream.

There was a clearing behind the house, and way off in the distance Tanner could see a section of the Great Smoky Mountains.

When she took him inside to see his room, he found the space clean, homey-looking, and the bathroom was equipped with an old-fashioned clawfoot bathtub. There was also a fireplace, although the weather was temperate.

"What do you think?" Susan said.

"Beautiful," Tanner said, as his eyes locked on hers.

Susan smiled. "I was talking about the room."

"It's very nice, and much better than a hotel room."

"I hope you like lasagna, because that's what I'm serving tonight."

"That sounds good."

"And oh yes, there's one other guest, but she's long-term. I'll introduce you two over dinner."

"What time is dinner?"

"Six-thirty, and you don't have to watch that small TV; there's a wide flat-screen in the living room."

"Thanks, but I'm more of a reader than a watcher."

"Me too, and I'll see you around."

"Thank you."

After Susan left, Tanner took off his jacket and tie, then he sat on the side of the bed to call Sammy.

"Where are you, Tanner?"

"There's been a change of plans. I'm staying at a bed & breakfast on Hooper Avenue."

"Why?"

"Better food," Tanner said, although he was hoping to appease other appetites with Susan Holmes.

"Should I come there?"

"You haven't checked in yet?"

"No, I ah, got delayed."

"Fine, then come here, and just say that someone recommended the place to you," Tanner told Sammy, then Sammy relayed the news about the biker club.

"I can see Bobby Volks as a drug dealer, so yeah, I'll check it out."

"Maybe I should go. I am the one with the motorcycle."

"Show up on a rented bike? You might as well ride a tricycle."

"All right, but you remember why we're here. Volks is mine."

"I hear you, Sammy, and I'll see you soon."

Tanner put away the phone and headed for the shower. On the way there, he spotted the door that connected his room to the one on the left. He opened it and found another door, which was locked.

He wondered if the room beyond the door belonged to Susan, and if so, would she make use of it to pay him a visit.

After leaving the door on his side unlocked, Tanner headed into the bathroom to get clean, while thinking dirty thoughts.

23

## SINNER OR SAINT?

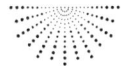

WILMINGTON, DELAWARE, ELEVEN YEARS EARLIER

"It's a con! It's got to be," Joe Pullo said, as he and Tanner watched Reverend Carlo Conti enter the women's shelter on Bennett Street. There was also a soup kitchen at the other end of the building, and a group of people were lined up outside for a free breakfast.

Tanner read from the shelter's brochure. "'The mission of the Teresa R. Rowen women's shelter is to prevent abuse, change families, and save lives.' How do you build a con out of that?"

"I don't know. Maybe he's turning the women out somehow."

"That's not what that madam said. She said Conti was the biggest pain in the ass she's ever known, and that he actually talked three of her girls into giving up the life."

Pullo rubbed a hand over his chin. "People don't

change, Tanner, and Conti, he killed an innocent woman, remember?"

"Yeah, so what do you want to do?"

Pullo said nothing for several seconds as he stared across the street. Conti had come back outside with a woman and child. The child was hugging him around the neck as if he were Santa Claus.

"I need to think about this... figure the con out."

"Why don't we talk to some of the other people who work there?"

"Nah, it might tip him off."

"I have another idea then, but it will cost you lunch at a good restaurant this afternoon."

"It's on Sam's dime, so what's your idea?"

THE REPORTER TURNED OUT TO BE A TALL BLONDE NAMED Cassidy. She was giving Tanner ideas, but she seemed to have eyes only for Pullo, whom she smiled at frequently. They had contacted her with the story that they represented a family trust that was looking for worthy charities to donate to in the Wilmington area.

"That women's shelter has done wonderful things," Cassidy told them. "I worked the crime beat in this city for three years, and I saw them save more than a few girls."

"The Reverend Conti, what do you know about him?"

"The girls working the streets love him. He beat up a pimp once and the cops looked the other way. I personally know a girl that he talked into going back home. After she graduated high school she went to work in the shelter, and at night she studies to be a lawyer."

"Still," Pullo said, "it seems odd, a man working inside

a women's shelter. Doesn't it bother the women who come there?"

Cassidy grinned. "You obviously haven't met Reverend Carlo; he's like a big teddy bear."

"Un-huh, anything else you can tell us?"

Cassidy leaned across the table. "I could tell you more over dinner, but just us, no offense to your friend."

"None taken," Tanner said, as he envied Pullo.

"Where should I pick you up?" Pullo asked, and Cassidy gave him her address.

After she left, Pullo saluted Tanner with his beer bottle.

"You're on your own tonight; I'll be pumping Cassidy."

"For information?" Tanner asked.

Pullo just smiled.

24

NO WAY TO TREAT A LADY

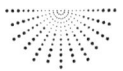

WILMINGTON, DELAWARE, ELEVEN YEARS EARLIER

With nothing else to do, Tanner staked out the women's shelter that night.

Pullo had the car, which placed Tanner on foot. He was wearing dark clothes with a hood, as he stayed back in the shadows of a burned-out building.

He saw Conti twice, and each time there was a child nearby who hugged the big man as if he were a kindly old grandfather. The shelter was in a bad neighborhood, but Tanner noticed that everyone who walked past Conti greeted him with a smile or showed respect, even the gangbangers.

If Conti were running a con, Tanner didn't know what it was.

After growing bored, he moved onto the sidewalk and began the trek back to the motel. When the same car drove past him twice and parked up ahead, he assumed it meant trouble.

He was carrying a gun, but he had seen at least two silhouettes in the car, and if there were as many as four, Tanner wanted to even the odds by using the element of surprise.

When the sidewalk curved and placed him in a blind spot to the men in the car, he left the street and began cutting through backyards as fast as he could. After traveling two houses farther down from where the car was parked, Tanner moved back toward the street and spotted two of the bodyguards from the whorehouse. They were both turned around in their seats and looking for him.

The driver was the man Pullo had struck with the ashtray, while the passenger had his right arm in a sling and was likely the man who had tumbled down the stairs and dislocated his shoulder.

Tanner cursed silently. This was a complication they didn't need. They had obviously followed him from the shelter and had plans for him. But had they just followed him, or had they followed both he and Pullo earlier?

Tanner slipped from the shadows and spoke when he was six feet away from the car.

"If either of you moves I'll light you up."

Both men twitched, but it was from surprise, and not an attempt to use their weapons. Afterwards, they slowly turned their heads to look at him.

"We just wanted to talk," said the driver, and Tanner saw the huge lump on his forehead that resulted from the ashtray hitting him.

"Let me see your hands."

The hands went up slowly. Tanner saw that the man in the passenger seat held a sawed-off shotgun in his left hand, while the driver carried a Beretta.

"I see how you were going to talk. Toss the weapons in the back seat, and then I want the driver to get out."

"Why just me?"

"Toss the guns. Do it now!"

The men followed instructions because they had little choice. By the time they turned to face Tanner, they would be dead.

Once the driver was out, Tanner had him stand in front of an overgrown hedge. Both men were dressed as he was, in dark clothing with a hood. The traffic was sporadic and there was no one in sight but the three of them; it wasn't the sort of neighborhood where many people traveled on foot at night.

"Are there men after my partner too?"

"We only saw you," said the man still sitting in the car.

He seemed to be telling the truth, which meant they had just picked up his trail. It also meant that Pullo was in the clear.

Tanner glanced into the car, saw the keys dangling in the ignition, and then shot the man in the passenger seat twice in the chest.

When he swiveled around, he saw that the driver had run to his left, but the man couldn't outrun a bullet, nor three of them.

Tanner was headed for the driver's side door before the punk's body had even settled. After checking to see that the other man had died, he pointed the car in the direction of the whorehouse.

THE BIG MAN WHO HAD PREVIOUSLY GREETED TANNER AND Pullo at the door came outside onto the home's porch, after having heard the car pull into the driveway.

Tanner was still in the car with the window rolled down, while his hood was up over his head. The face of the dead man propped up beside him was lost in shadow, but the coppery scent of his blood was cloying in the confines of the car.

When the huge thug walked over to the car, Tanner was leaning over as if he were trying to get something out of the glove compartment. With no white skin showing, the man mistook him for one of the other guards.

The big man leaned on the windowsill and Tanner felt the car sink toward the ground from his weight.

"Yo, brothers, did you find them two assholes?"

"They found one of them," Tanner said, even as he used his left hand to jam a long knife up under the man's chin, through the soft palate of his mouth, and into his brain.

The man made a high-pitched sound that was incongruous with his huge frame, toppled backwards onto the lawn, rolled, and finally settled at the base of a rose bush. Tanner never bothered to check if he was dead but left the car to walk up the stairs and lean beside the door.

It took nearly five minutes, but then the door opened, and the madam stuck her head out. She was dressed all in red again. Tanner idly wondered if it was the only color she ever wore.

When she spotted Tanner, a look of recognition lit her face, right before Tanner smashed his gun against her forehead. She staggered out onto the porch, spun around once, and fell on her ass. There came the sound of heavy footfalls, followed by a hoarse voice filled with surprise.

"Emily, what happened?"

It was the fourth guard, the one he had kicked in the throat. The man rushed outside, bent over to help the madam up, but then spotted Tanner.

"Oh shit."

"Oh yeah," Tanner said, and shot the man in the head.

The madam looked up at him, her eyes still glassy.

"You wouldn't hurt a lady, would you?"

"No, not a lady," Tanner said, and shot her between the eyes.

After pulling the body from the passenger seat, Tanner got back behind the wheel and drove off.

25

ANGELS AND BAD BOYS

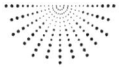

Hanna apologized for how rundown the motor home was, but Merle and Earl told her that it was better than most of the places they had stayed at over the years.

That started a conversation about traveling, and the boys discovered that the girls were as well traveled as they were.

"Oh yeah, we've been all over the country. See, Savannah and me are singers and musicians; well, we were, but we got tired of the road and came home to settle down. We grew up right down the road in Kellyville."

"Let's hear you sing," Earl said.

The girls looked bashful for a moment, but then began singing a familiar country song. They had good voices, and Merle and Earl were enraptured.

"You two should be on stage at the Grand Ole Opry."

Hanna giggled. "Oh Merle, you're so easy to please."

The four of them looked at each other silently, and then Hanna pointed back toward the house.

"It's gettin' late; we'll see you boys in the mornin'."

Savannah leaned over and kissed Earl on the cheek. "Sweet dreams."

"You too, Miss Cole."

When the girls were gone, Earl turned to look at his brother. "I think I'm fallin' in love."

"I don't blame you, and let me tell ya, I like that Hanna too."

"Merle, we have to think of some way to help them. I don't mean give them the house, but we can't send 'em packin' either."

"Yeah, let me sleep on it."

The boys lay down for the night but were too excited to fall asleep right away.

"Merle, you awake?"

"Yeah."

"They sang like angels, didn't they?"

"Better," Merle said.

IN TENNESSEE, SUSAN'S OTHER GUEST TURNED OUT TO BE Amy, the cop who had pulled Sammy over.

She was surprised to see Sammy, but also looked pleased. Over dinner, they told the story of how they met, as Tanner and Sammy pretended to be strangers.

Tanner showed interest in her story about the drug-dealing bikers. When he asked her what Calabrese looked like, the description fit Bobby Volks.

"Calabrese sounds Italian," Tanner remarked, and Susan shook her head.

"He has a slight accent, but it's not Italian; I'd say it's more Slavic."

"I thought that meth would be a big city problem," Sammy said. "How long has this been going on?"

"The meth dealing is new," Amy said. "But the chief says that Calabrese has been a problem for years. He owns the Iron Horse; it's a bar on the west end of town that used to be a small warehouse. Those bikers have taken the place over."

"Calabrese wants my pub too," Susan said. "He made me an offer just last week. It wasn't even half what the business is worth."

After dinner, Sammy went out on the front porch to call Sophia while Amy went to see her boyfriend, and Tanner joined Susan in the kitchen for coffee.

"What sort of work do you do, Tom?"

"I'm a freelance researcher."

Susan laughed.

"What's so funny?"

"I had you pegged as a Federal Agent working undercover."

"If I was, a researcher would be a good cover."

"No fair, now I don't know what to think."

After another few sips of coffee, Susan asked a question. "Were you recently divorced?"

"No, why?"

"I don't know; you just have that look, like you're a bit adrift."

"I guess I am, but being around new scenery helps, and I'm enjoying your company."

Susan was a widow whose husband had been a Marine. The active-duty officer had died in a training accident three years earlier.

Tanner talked with her about books for a while and found that Susan was well-read. She also spoke Spanish and French and had taught both languages while a high school teacher.

"You must have been a young teacher."

Susan smiled. "I was twenty-eight, and that was eighteen years ago."

"You do not look your age."

"I stay busy and it keeps me young."

They moved into the living room and Susan put on an old western, Winchester '73 with Jimmy Stewart.

Five minutes into the movie, Tanner leaned over and kissed Susan. She kissed him back, and by the time Stewart got his man, Tanner had gotten his woman, and spent the rest of the night in Susan's arms.

26

OOPS!

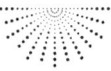

Susan ran a hand over Tanner's chest. They were both naked and had just made love again after waking.

"My late husband had been wounded in combat twice, and he had less scars than you. Exactly what sort of research do you do?"

"The dangerous kind."

Susan stared into his eyes. "Your name is not really Tom Myers, is it?"

"Susan, if I was what you think I am, then I wouldn't be able to answer that question, would I?"

She kissed him. "You just did."

She rose from the bed and Tanner enjoyed the sight of her nakedness. He had been with older women before and always found them less inhibited than their younger counterparts. Susan wasn't without flaws, but she knew they didn't define or detract from her overall beauty. That self-confidence was arousing in its own right.

"I'm going to shower. Would you like to save water?"

Tanner answered her by standing, and when Susan looked down, she smiled.

"Whoever you are, you have great recuperative powers."

Tanner placed his hands on her hips. "You inspire me."

Susan pushed him back onto the bed, then climbed aboard.

"We'll shower later."

~

BY THE TIME THEY MADE IT DOWNSTAIRS, AMY HAD already cooked breakfast. She greeted the two of them with a knowing smile.

Sammy was seated at the table eating. He sent Susan and Tanner a wave while his mouth was full of buttermilk biscuit.

"Amy, you're a guest here, remember?"

"I don't mind cooking sometimes, Susan. And you and I both know that you could charge me more than you do."

Susan kissed Amy on the cheek. "I like your company, and thank you for cooking."

Susan's phone rang while she was doing the dishes. As she listened to her caller, her expression grew worried.

"That was Millie; she opened up The Roundup today for the breakfast crowd. She told me that there are two bikers scaring away the customers."

"What are they doing?" Amy asked.

"Nothing, they're just parked out front on those bikes of theirs, but you know how most of them look, they're scary looking."

Amy grabbed her gun belt and strapped it on. "I'll come with you, Susan."

"I'll come along too," Tanner said.

Susan spoke to Sammy. "Oh Jack, there's an older woman named Carrie who watches the place for me during the day. She should be here any minute if you need something while I'm at the bar."

Sammy thanked her but said that he'd tag along to get a look at the bikers. As they were leaving, he whispered to Tanner.

"Are we going to need the guns?"

"I doubt it," Tanner whispered back. "There are only two of them."

"Amy's the law; maybe she'll scare them off."

Tanner nodded, but law or not, Amy was a small woman. She also had rules of conduct she had to adhere to; Tanner had no such restrictions.

AMY HAD LEFT FIRST, WITH SAMMY FOLLOWING BEHIND ON his bike. So when Tanner and Susan arrived, Amy was already talking to the bikers, as Sammy stood by and watched.

The bikers were a scruffy pair, with long dirty beards and wild hair. They both wore leather jackets even though the day was warm.

They ignored Amy after they pointed out to her that they were legally parked in front of meters and had paid for their time. If they wanted to, they could sit there all day.

Tanner decided to make that option seem less appealing.

After telling Sammy to distract Amy, he walked past the men to the rear of the second bike and kicked it hard. The bike toppled over onto the sidewalk and cracked the mirror on that side. As Amy spun around to see what had happened, Tanner smiled at the bikers.

"Oops, sorry guys; I must have bumped into it."

Tanner was dressed in chinos and a blue polo shirt. He was clean-shaven, had the look of a tourist, and the bikers didn't consider him a threat. The man whose bike was damaged moved toward him, and as he drew near, he reached out for Tanner.

Tanner grabbed the man's wrist with both hands, turned, and flipped the biker onto his back. The man thudded atop the sidewalk with his skull taking much of the impact.

When Tanner turned to face the second man, he saw him bringing out a knife. A quick kick disarmed him. It was followed by a sweep kick that took the man's feet out from under him.

Amy stood above the man with her gun drawn and told him to stay down, while Sammy pointed at the bikers and used Tanner's phony name.

"They tried to assault Mr. Myers."

"That's how I see it too," Amy said.

"I won't press charges if they leave," Tanner told her. When he looked over at Susan, he saw that she had her arms folded across her chest and was smiling at him.

The second biker helped his companion up. Although the man appeared a bit dazed, he was able to mount his bike and ride away.

After Amy drove off to the police station, and Sammy rode away on his bike, Susan gave Tanner a kiss on the lips.

"You're here for Calabrese, aren't you?"

"I'll just say this; by the time I leave here, he'll no longer be a problem."

Susan took Tanner by the hand, and they went inside the pub.

## 27
# BEES DO IT, BIRDS DO IT

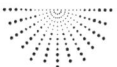

Merle and Earl were working harder than they had in a good long time, as they helped Hanna and Savannah around the farm.

The chores were familiar ones, milking a cow, feeding chickens, weeding the garden, and mending a fence. However, they were both worn out by the end of the afternoon. Earl asked if it'd be all right if he took a soak in the tub.

"It's really your house, Earl, and you boys were a lot of help today," Hanna said.

While Earl went up to soak, Merle showered in the RV. After changing into fresh clothes, he walked back to the house to sit on a porch swing.

Hanna came out onto the porch. After taking a seat beside him, she handed Merle a can of beer.

"Dinner is ready, and we can eat anytime you want."

"What are we havin'? It smells great."

"Fried chicken, yams, cornbread stuffing, spinach, and Savannah baked a peach cobbler."

"Lordy, my mouth's waterin' just hearin' about it."

"Have you figured out what you wanna do with us yet?"

"Whaddya mean?"

"I mean are you kickin' us off the property?"

"No! Hell no, you got taken, and yeah, the place isn't really yours, but me and Earl can see all the work and money you ladies put into it. It would be just plain mean to kick you out."

"Were you two thinkin' of moving back here?"

Merle smiled. "We weren't, but when I look at this view, enjoyin' the quiet, I wonder why we ever left."

"I um, I wouldn't mind if you stayed. It's nice havin' men around, and Savannah has a thing for your brother."

"Is that a fact?"

"It is."

"Now that's funny."

"Why?"

"I got a thing for her sister."

Hanna grinned, and Merle leaned over and kissed her.

EARL HAD BEEN LYING BACK IN THE TUB ENJOYING HIS WARM soapy bath when the door opened, and Savannah stepped in.

"Miss Cole?"

"Call me Savannah, Earl."

After swallowing, Earl said, "All right, Savannah."

He had brought clean clothes into the bath with him and placed them on the closed lid of the toilet seat. Savannah scooped them up and turned to leave.

"Where are you goin' with my clothes?"

"You got a button loose on your shirt. I'll take it to my bedroom and mend it."

"Oh, okay, but why take the pants?"

Savannah tugged hard on a belt loop and tore it loose.

"I gotta fix this here too."

Earl swallowed again, and it was followed by a smile.

"If you want your clothes back, my bedroom is the door on the right."

"Um, okay."

"Don't be long now."

He wasn't, he dried himself faster than he ever had before and left the bathroom wearing only a towel, and a smile.

28

# EASY RIDER

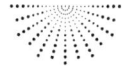

Tanner knew Sammy was growing restless, but if Bobby Volks was Calabrese, he had a group of bikers around him.

That meant they had to separate him from his men and get him alone, as it would be their best chance to kill him.

Tanner had stayed at Susan's pub all day in case more trouble came. She worked there until five o'clock, and was headed home to cook dinner, when she spotted a friend. The man's name was Garrett Bates. He was bald, black, about fifty, and ran the town newspaper.

Tanner had read several back issues of the paper, The Rainberry Gazette, while he waited for Susan, and knew that Bates was no fan of Calabrese. The front-page story the week before had been about Calabrese's bar and all the trouble the place bred for the town. He also insinuated that Calabrese was behind the area's growing meth problem.

Bates had a firm grip, and he used it when he shook Tanner's hand. "Mr. Myers, it's good to meet you, and you're a lucky man to be enjoying Susan's… cooking."

Tanner studied Bates and saw a hint of jealousy. If he had detected that Tanner was Susan's lover, he was perceptive.

"She's a great cook."

"Yes, indeed, and I also heard that you got into a scuffle with a pair of bikers, is that true?"

"They overacted when I bumped into one of their bikes."

"You must be clumsy," Bates said, and after saying goodbye, he went inside the pub.

"I sense that there's history between you two," Tanner told Susan.

"As friends only, although, he often asks for more."

"I don't blame him."

There was a green panel van parked at the curb with the name of the town's newspaper painted on the side in yellow. The van had no windows in the rear and the rest were heavily tinted.

"He delivers his own newspapers, I see," Tanner said.

"The paper only comes out once a week. The latest copy I have is last week's news."

Tanner sighed. "I guess that means I missed the bake sale at the church."

THEY RETURNED TO THE HOUSE, WHERE THEY FOUND Sammy coming back from a run. Sammy wore gray shorts and a red sleeveless T-shirt, with blue & white sneakers.

As Susan went inside to cook dinner, Tanner talked to Sammy.

"If I know my thugs, Calabrese won't let what happened this morning go by without trying to retaliate, so stay sharp."

"I will, but we need to find out if Calabrese is really Bobby Volks."

"I was going to do that tonight."

"Without me?"

"No, you'll be coming along to create a diversion, and then I'll—"

The rumble of motorcycles filled the air. The three bikes turned the corner and headed toward them. The rider of the first motorcycle was huge. After rounding the corner, the two men with him stayed back, and the lead rider pulled up in front of Susan's house.

"Be cool," Tanner whispered, knowing what was coming next.

And when the man removed his helmet, the face revealed belonged to Bobby Volks.

## 29

## A CHANGED MAN

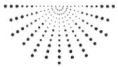

WILMINGTON, DELAWARE, ELEVEN YEARS EARLIER

The morning after the attack on the brothel, Pullo looked impressed by Tanner's news. They were in Pullo's motel room.

"You killed them all?"

"I had to, Joe; otherwise, they would have kept coming."

"Yeah, they knew we were interested in Conti, so they staked out the shelter. But Tanner, you took a risk doing it alone."

"I've killed more than that by myself before. Did you learn anything new about Conti last night?"

"Yeah, the man's a saint now, or so it seems."

"What's our next move?"

"I want to confront him and see how he reacts."

"If he's a fake running a con of some kind, he'll run."

"Yeah, but he won't get far."

"He walks to that shelter, so he must live nearby," Tanner said.

"He does, somewhere three or four blocks east of it, according to Cassidy."

"Do you want to go look for him now?"

"Yeah, and maybe we can end things and head back to New York."

They left Pullo's room, and Tanner stared over at the man guarding the door across the way. It was a different man than the first. He eyed Tanner and Pullo with suspicion.

"Before we leave here, I want to know what's in that room," Tanner said.

"I don't blame you; they've got me curious too."

They were on their way to find Carlo Conti's apartment when they spotted him walking down the street toward the shelter.

Pullo circled around, and when Conti reached the next corner, Tanner approached Conti from the front, as Pullo came up behind him and spoke.

"Carlo, Sam Giacconi sends his regards."

Carlo Conti was huge. Tanner thought he looked taller than the six-foot-six he was reported to be.

The big man sighed. "I guess the Lord is calling me home now. But please, not here in the street, not where the children can see."

Tanner and Pullo exchanged glances. The man didn't seem afraid to die but was only concerned that a child might view the violence. Before they could say another word, two teenage boys came out of the hallway of an apartment house, and one of them was carrying a knife.

"Reverend Conti, are these two bothering you?"

Conti's face grew red with anger. "Hakeem, what are you doing with that knife?"

The boy looked down at his hand, then pointed at Pullo and Tanner.

"They look like trouble."

"There will be trouble if I catch you with a knife again."

"I'm sorry, Rev."

"All right then, but you and Randy go inside and eat breakfast; school starts in an hour."

Hakeem hung his head. "My moms is drunk again, Rev."

"Go down to the soup kitchen and tell Kelli I sent you, she'll feed you boys," Conti said, and then he looked at Pullo and Tanner. "And let her know that I might be late."

Hakeem handed Conti the knife and the big man broke the cheap blade in two and tossed the pieces down the sewer drain.

"Could we take this back to my apartment? Boys like those two don't need to see more violence."

"We're just talking," Pullo said. "We want to know what the con is."

Carlo Conti laughed, and the booming sound of it filled the air.

"There's no con, friend. The Carlo Conti they sent you to kill is gone. He died the day he killed Teresa Silva."

Pullo cocked his head. "That's the woman you murdered, Tony Silva's wife."

"Before she married Tony Silva, she was Teresa Bondi, and Teresa Bondi was the only woman I ever loved."

"I don't get it," Pullo said.

"Teresa and I grew up in the same neighborhood and she was my girlfriend, but she came to despise my violent streak and she refused to marry me. That only made me meaner, although I never stopped loving her."

"Then why did you kill her?" Tanner asked.

Conti looked skyward, as tears filled his eyes. "I was all coked up and full of hate that day. Tony Silva wasn't even a hood, he was a jeweler, but the rumor was that he kept cash in the house. I broke in there and fired at the bed without even looking at them, and when… when I, oh God, Teresa. I didn't even notice that it was Teresa, not until I had filled my pockets with money and jewelry from a lock box Silva kept on his dresser. I killed her, I killed the only person I ever loved, and as God is my witness, it drove me mad."

"Is that what you call this Father Flanagan act, madness?" Pullo said.

Conti wiped the tears from his eyes. "Think what you want, but it's no act."

A young black woman called out Conti's name from across the street and waved with a smile. She then crossed over with her two little girls, and the kids ran to Conti. When the big man bent over, the little girls each kissed him on the cheek.

"Good morning, Reverend; I wish I could stop and talk, but I have to drop these two off at daycare and then get to work."

"I understand, Gloria, but stop by the shelter sometime soon."

"I'll do that, goodbye."

After the woman moved on with her children, Conti continued his story.

"I crawled into a bottle and lived like a bum on the streets of Philly for five years before coming down here. That's when I met a man who changed my life. He got me help, sobered me up, and he told me I could change. He said I didn't have to stay who I was, that I could help others, and that I could be forgiven any sin."

"I guess he never met Sam Giacconi, because Sam is not the forgiving type."

Conti smiled at Pullo. "You can't scare me, so don't even try. If it's my time, so be it."

After saying that, Conti walked off toward the clinic.

Pullo stared at Tanner. "What the hell do you make of that?"

"I think he's for real."

"He's still Carlo Conti, and Sam sent us here to kill him."

"No, Joe. Sam sent *you* here to kill Conti. He sent me here to back you up, and I will, no matter what call you make."

Pullo hung his head. "There's only one call, Tanner. I do what Sam asks me to do."

"He asked you to kill an animal, a son of a bitch, and that's not Conti, not anymore."

"We'll watch him and see if he runs."

"And if he doesn't?"

Pullo grimaced and started walking. "The car is back this way."

Tanner followed without a word, then waited to see what Pullo would do.

30

# THE MAN HIMSELF

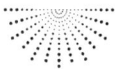

"You're Myers, hmm? I thought you'd be bigger."

"I hear that a lot," Tanner said.

Calabrese, who was really Bobby Volks, was a large man dressed all in leather. He wore a full beard that showed hints of gray, and his brown hair was as long as Sammy's raven hair, but it looked greasy and uncombed. When his flinty eyes left Tanner, he stared over at Sammy and spoke to him with his gravelly voice.

"Who are you?"

"You can call me Sammy."

"Well, Sammy, why don't you run along, kid?"

"Why don't you make me?"

Tanner shot Sammy a warning look. This was neither the time nor place to kill Volks and provoking him might make him aggressive.

Volks laughed at Sammy. "I remember being your age. I thought I could kick anybody's ass, but I couldn't, kid, and neither can you."

"Why are you here?" Tanner said.

"Let me introduce myself, I'm Johnny Calabrese. I'm

always looking for good men, and anybody who could take on two of my guys and not get a scratch is a good man."

"The two at the restaurant this morning were trying to get by on ugly. It works with most people, but not with me."

"Goddamn if I don't like you, Myers. And with those clean good looks you can go places my other guys can't. I'll pay you two grand a week, what do you say?"

"Why don't I come out to that bar of yours and talk? It's somewhat public here, you know?"

"I hear you, come by at ten."

"Sammy comes too."

"Is he old enough to drink?"

"Does it matter?"

"Not at my place. Hell, we had these two high school girls there last week. You should see the things they'll do with the right incentive."

"Such as free meth?"

Volks grinned. "We're getting ahead of ourselves; we'll talk business tonight." Volks jammed his helmet on his hairy head, revved up his bike, and peeled away.

Sammy spat on the ground. "If I had my gun, I would have killed him."

"And then you would be sitting in a jail cell. We do this smart or not at all. Do you understand me?"

"I get you, but I don't like it."

"You will, because in the end, Volks dies."

Susan came running out of the house. "Was that Calabrese?"

"Yeah. He invited Jack and me to his bar."

"What? You're not going, are you?"

"I'm going, and I'll be fine."

Susan looked back and forth at Tanner and Sammy.

"Could you two stop playacting for a moment and at least tell me your real names?"

Sammy stared at Tanner with a surprised expression. "You told her we were working together?"

"I didn't have to; Susan is smart. My name is Tanner, he's Sammy."

Susan studied Tanner. "Yes, that name fits you better, and there's no first name either, is there?"

"He's like Cher or Madonna," Sammy said.

Susan kissed Tanner on the cheek, then turned to go inside. "I have to get back to my food, and I'll keep your secret."

They watched her go, then Tanner asked Sammy about Amy.

"What about her? There's nothing going on between us if that's what you're asking? I wouldn't cheat on Sophia."

"Relax, that's not what I meant. But I do want you to talk to Amy and find out more about the meth business, particularly about how difficult it's been to discover how Calabrese is transporting it. I got the impression that the cops think it's the bikers."

"They do; it's why she was so rough on me when she pulled me over. But every time they check one of them, they're clean. Amy said that before meth hit the streets, their biggest problem was homegrown pot."

Tanner stared at Sammy. "Tonight is just reconnaissance. I want to see the inside of that bar. Susan said that Volks lives there, and maybe that's where we'll kill him."

"What if it's a trap and he just wants payback for what you did to his guys?"

"I'll change his mind."

"You're a cocky bastard, Tanner."

"Yes, I hear that a lot too."

~

As they ate dinner, Tanner asked Amy about Calabrese. A concerned expression formed on her face.

"Understand something, the man has been charged with no crimes and everything I tell you is just hearsay and guesswork."

"I'm not a judge and this isn't a courtroom; I just want to get a better sense of the man."

"Why?" Amy said.

Susan answered her. "Tom's a researcher. I guess it just makes him naturally nosey."

"Oh, but you might not want to stick your nose into Calabrese's business. It's not healthy."

"He's hurt someone?"

"Nothing we can prove, but before Calabrese came to town the local thugs were three brothers named Dobbs. They ran the pot trade, some cocaine maybe, and definitely some girls. Allegedly, Calabrese tried to buy his way in and was refused, and no one has seen the Dobbs brothers since, and now we think Calabrese is running things."

"Tell them about Kevin Ryan, Amy," Susan said.

"Kevin Ryan was a town council member and a part-time preacher. He was determined to run Calabrese and his bikers out of town and he would badmouth them to everyone. One day after church, Mr. Ryan just disappeared."

"Like the Dobbs brothers disappeared?" Sammy said.

"There have been others too; it seems that Calabrese doesn't like to be criticized," Susan said.

"What about Garrett Bates?" Tanner asked. "He seems to be going after Calabrese in that paper of his."

Amy lit up in a smile. "He's a brave man, Mr. Bates is. The chief has asked all of us deputies to watch out for him."

"I see," Tanner said.

∽

When it was time for him to visit Calabrese, Susan kissed Tanner goodbye.

"Try not to acquire any new scars, okay?"

"Don't wait up; I don't know how long this might take."

"I won't be able to sleep until you get back, and you'll find me in your bed."

"Talk about in-room amenities."

Susan laughed, then grew serious. "Be safe, Tanner."

"Count on it."

As they were driving away, Sammy made an observation. "Susan really likes you, and she's a good woman."

"That she is," Tanner said, and they went off to see Bobby Volks.

31

THE OFFER OF A LIFETIME

After eating a late dinner, Savannah brought out a Twister mat, and she, Earl, Hanna, and Merle played the game until they collapsed on top of each other in a pile, while laughing.

The two couples then sat around talking, and the girls asked about New York. When they learned that Merle and Earl had driven for Johnny Rossetti, they seemed impressed.

"He was famous," Hanna said. "I remember hearin' about him."

Earl sniffled. "I liked him a lot. He let us both drive him around even though he only needed one chauffeur."

"And you say your sister is marryin' this other fella, Joe?"

"Yeah, and he's not as nice as Johnny was, but he treats Laurel Lee like a queen, and that's all that matters," Merle said.

"Hanna and me went to New York about five years ago, and Lordy was it ever a busy place. I couldn't live there, not for always. I like farm life better."

"Merle," Hanna said. "Why did you and Earl leave here?"

"We were gonna get rich, but instead, we just drifted around."

"You could stay here, for a while at least."

Merle looked over at his brother. "What do you think, Earl?"

Earl reached over and took Savannah's hand. "I can't think of anywhere else I'd rather be."

Hanna smiled. "All righty then."

The sound of a car came from outside, prompting them to all rise and look out the window. It was the chief of police; he was dressed in civilian clothes and was stepping out of a blue SUV. There was a man with him; the man wore a suit and carried a laptop case.

They strolled out onto the porch and Hanna greeted the men.

"Hey there, Chief, is somethin' up?"

The chief smiled and gestured at the other man, who was trim, with a scalp going bald in the middle.

"Hi folks, sorry to call so late, but it's good news. This here is Mr. Wilson. He represents some people that would like to buy the farm from you."

"Buy it? How much?" Merle said.

Mr. Wilson mentioned a number that made the Carter brothers and Cole sisters gape at him in surprise.

"That's a lot of money," Savannah said.

"The people I represent are looking to build new housing and a shopping center. This is a good area for the project."

Hanna shook her head. "Some folks tried that last year. They bought up that swampland to the north and took to drainin' it, but it cost more than they thought. By the time they got the swamp drained, they wound up goin' broke."

Wilson smiled. "I'm well aware of that, because I acquired that land for a song after they did all the work. They quit too early because they ran out of financial backing, but a little more effort will make that parcel viable. If we add your farm to it, we'll be able to proceed right away."

Wilson walked up the steps and handed out cards with the amount he was willing to pay written on the back. "Think about it for a day or two and then let me know."

Hanna took a card and smiled at Wilson. "Would you like to come inside and have some iced tea or coffee?"

"No ma'am, but thank you. I've taken enough of your time."

They all said goodnight to Wilson and the chief, and then stood looking at each other.

"Merle, are you gonna sell?" Hanna asked.

"I don't know, but if we did, we could give you back all the money you lost and still have a bundle."

"But then we'd have no farm and no place to live," Savannah said.

Merle looked at his brother. "What do you think?"

"I think we should sleep on it, and besides, we gotta call Laurel Lee and ask her about it too."

"Yeah," Merle said.

Hanna looked sad as she opened the screen door, but then she looked back at Merle.

"You would really give us our money back?"

"Sure, it would be fair with all the work you did here."

Hanna let the screen door shut and went to Merle. "You're a good man, do you know that?"

Merle thought about it a second and said, "No."

Hanna laughed as she took Merle's hand. "No more sleeping in the RV for you."

Merle sent her a silly grin, then he followed her inside, as Earl walked along with Savannah.

## 32

## ...NOR IRON BARS A CAGE

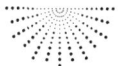

A BIKER ROUGHLY THE SIZE OF A REFRIGERATOR GREETED Tanner and Sammy as they walked into the Iron Horse bar. Calabrese called over and told the man to let them pass.

Both Tanner and Sammy were armed, but then, so were the bikers. The interior of the bar was better lit than Tanner would have guessed. There were a dozen or more fluorescent light fixtures hanging from the ceiling of the A-frame building, which had once been a carpet warehouse. Windows lined the walls on each side, but they were high up off the floor, and several showed cracks, while the bar itself smelled of spilt beer and sour sweat.

There were several women in the bar. They were all wearing short skirts and plunging necklines. One particular beauty with a front tooth missing flicked her tongue at Sammy as they walked by.

"I think she likes you."

"I'm taken," Sammy told Tanner, and then winced.

Tanner ignored the remark, knowing that Sammy

meant no harm by it, then he concentrated on filing away details about the bar's interior.

Calabrese left his barstool and gestured for them to follow him, as he headed toward the rear of the rectangular building with two of his biggest men flanking him.

The floor of the old building creaked beneath their feet with each step. The creaking was felt and not heard, as the jukebox blasted country music and raucous voices echoed off the walls.

As they walked down a short hallway, Tanner saw a windowless room with a brass bed in it. There was a blonde girl lying on the bed. She was topless, even younger than Sammy, and when Tanner looked into her blue eyes, he saw that she was high on something.

"That's Sissy; if you want a piece I can arrange it."

"I'll pass," Tanner said.

At the end of the hall was a door. There were crates full of empty bottles piled in front of it, which blocked the exit. Calabrese turned right just before reaching it and entered an office. There was an old wooden desk and a green metal filing cabinet, while a bare incandescent bulb hung from the ceiling, and bars were bolted across the room's lone window.

Calabrese, who was really Bobby Volks, sat in the chair behind the desk, as his two soldiers took positions in front of the window and leaned back against the bars.

Tanner stood to the left of the desk and gestured for Sammy to stand to the right of it. Sammy was perplexed by Tanner's request, but he complied.

Volks smiled up at them. "No offense but lift your shirts and turn around so I can see if you're wired."

They both complied, and Volks took note of the puckered wound on Tanner's chest.

"Somebody came close to putting you down, didn't they?"

"Close doesn't count."

"True, now here's the deal, two grand a week and you help me get rid of the competition. There's a group the next town over that's proving to be difficult. Real hillbillies, like a clan, and even their damn women and kids know how to shoot."

"They sell meth?"

"They grow and sell pot, and they must be doing two million a year easy. I don't know what they spend the money on, but it's not dental work, I can tell you that."

"I'll pass, and two grand a week is chump change."

Volks spread his arms wide. "Name a number."

"A hundred percent. You see, I'd rather take you down and run my own meth through here."

Volks pounded the desk with a fist, and Tanner was pleased to see that Sammy didn't flinch.

"Who are you working for, Myers?"

"You'll find out when the time comes."

Volks smiled. "Or maybe I'll find out when they send the next guy... after I kill you."

Tanner tossed his head toward the two leaning back against the bars.

"By the time those two clear their weapons I'll kill them, and if you reach for the shotgun bolted beneath the desk I'll feed it to you."

Volks cursed and pointed at the desktop, where the tops of two bolts were visible.

"It is sloppy work, isn't it? But you're the first one to spot the bolts."

Sammy nodded. He hadn't noticed them. If not for Tanner, he'd be standing directly in front of the gun.

Tanner tossed a thumb back at the doorway. "What's

the deal? You have a signal to let the men in the bar know that we can leave?"

Volks grinned. "Damn, I wish you worked for me."

One of the men leaning at the window straightened up, and both Sammy and Tanner drew their guns.

"Don't try it, and Calabrese, why don't you stand up. Sammy, get their guns, then check the hall."

Sammy collected the weapons, ducked low, and peered around the doorframe with one eye.

"It's clear."

"It's also the only way out of here," Volks said. "If you try moving those crates away from the back door, someone will spot you."

Sammy whispered to Tanner. "Why don't I kill him now?"

"Too many witnesses," Tanner whispered back.

"You have a plan to get out of here?"

"We're leaving by the window."

"What about the bars?"

"Calabrese," Tanner said in a normal voice. "Tell your gorillas to tear those bars off the window."

"They're bolted into the wall."

Tanner grinned. "If those bars aren't off in one minute, I start shooting."

"You're bluffing. That would bring the others running back here."

Tanner walked around the desk and placed his gun beneath Volks' chin. "Look in my eyes and tell me again that I'm bluffing."

Several seconds passed, and then Volks spoke to his men. "Jake, Ronny, tear those damn bars off the window."

"One side at a time," Tanner said. "It'll go easier."

The bikers did as they were told and the bars came off the window with much grunting and straining. While they were doing that, Tanner and Volks stared at each other without blinking.

Once the window was opened, Sammy climbed out, followed by the bikers, then Volks, and Tanner.

They walked together toward the front and found the parking lot empty. Everyone was inside waiting to hear the blast of the shotgun beneath the desk, or to see the emergence of the group from the office. Once they reached Tanner's rental, he put his gun away and spoke to Volks.

"Thanks for the hospitality."

"This is my territory and I won't give it up without a fight."

Sammy started the car and sped away as if he were being chased by demons.

"What if they follow us?"

"It's too public for him. He likes to make people disappear like magic, but keep an eye out anyway."

"So, what's our next move?"

"Tomorrow night we rob their meth shipment."

"What? How?"

"By playing a hunch. If I'm right, we'll have Volks right where we want him."

"And then he'll be the one that disappears?"

"By your hand, are you up to it?"

Sammy turned his head and Tanner saw the murder in his eyes.

"Good man."

## 33

## ONE CALL DOES IT ALL

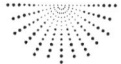

In Manhattan, Krupin looked out at the lights of the city from a penthouse suite, which was rented by Juan Alvarado under an alias.

Alvarado was on the phone with his father, and although Krupin didn't speak Spanish, he had heard his name mentioned twice. When the call ended, Juan Alvarado joined him on the balcony.

"The specialists were delayed, but they will be arriving soon, and then your troubles will be over."

"These specialists, they're going to kill Pullo and Tanner?"

"No, Tanner only. Pullo will be handled by more traditional methods."

"Such as?"

Alvarado smiled. "We're going to shoot him down like a dog in the street."

"I wish I could be there. I don't know how the hell he survived that fire."

"Before the call came through, you were telling me about a federal agent."

"His name is Ivanov. My people tell me he and his partner discovered that I went to Mexico. If that's true, they might also know you're here."

Juan smiled. "Many people were given money so that your government won't know I'm here, and yet, leaks still happen. Perhaps we can pay this FBI man of yours to go away."

"He's not the type, he likes to bust balls. I was thinking about another option. His partner is young and beautiful, maybe we could frame him for her murder, you know, make it look like a lover's quarrel."

"Are they lovers?"

"I have no idea, but an older man, younger woman, people would buy it. And I would love to see him put in his place."

Juan patted Krupin on the shoulder. "I like you, Michael; you're a man who knows how to hate creatively. Perhaps we'll visit that plan someday. For now, let's concentrate on Pullo and Tanner."

"Okay, but man I hate that Fed."

They sat and looked out at the skyline as they drank. When Juan stared at Krupin, the Russian felt the weight of the Mexican's gaze.

"Why are you staring?"

"My father is taking a risk in backing you. You do understand that, correct?"

"I understand that he'll be getting fifty percent for his trouble."

"The money is nothing compared to the risk. He's doing this behind the backs of the other cartels. If we fail here, this will give our enemies ammunition against us, but if we succeed, then we'll be able to dictate terms for future American cities."

"I thought you were already in America. I know you guys are supplying drugs everywhere."

"True, but it's… what's the word, underground? By backing you openly we'll be sending up a flag."

"New York City is worth the risk. Controlling the ports alone is worth billions over the long haul."

"Yes, and you and I, we are both young men, and it's the young men who usher in new ages. Once we have a strong grip on New York, then we move across the sea to Europe and make alliances there, and after that, Asia."

Krupin grinned. "You're ambitious, that's good, so am I, and I never thought that Pullo would be so hard to kill."

Juan waved a dismissive hand. "He will die soon enough. Pullo isn't old, but he's not young either. It's time for him to go."

"I'm more worried about Tanner."

"That one intrigues my father, and I know that he would like to own him, but since you say that he and Pullo are friends, it would be too dangerous to keep him around."

"You have to kill him. I don't know who these specialists are that you have coming here, but they'd better not fail."

"They never have. In the end, no matter how highly skilled he may be, Tanner is just a man, and a man can be killed. But now enough talk of men. Why don't you order up some women? After all, this is your city."

Krupin grinned. "I just have to make a call, any preference?"

"Blonde, I love natural blondes, my friend."

"I'll get two for you," Krupin said, and wondered how friendly the man would be if he knew he had slept with his mother.

## 34
## A VERY BAD MAN

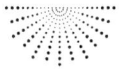

Tanner decided that it would be a good idea to keep watch, so he and Sammy took turns.

Tanner had taken the first shift, and after Sammy came down to relieve him at three a.m., he went up, took a quick shower, and crawled into bed beside Susan.

"Oohh, you're cold."

"Sorry," Tanner said. "And I was trying not to wake you."

Susan took him in her arms. "Come here and let me warm you up."

Tanner felt the softness of her curves against him. He reached up and caressed her face.

"That might do more than warm me up."

Susan smiled. "That's the plan."

They made love, and when it was over, Susan lay back in his arms.

"I know this won't last, and that you'll be leaving, but I want you to know that it's more than just sex to me. I'm too old for just sex; I need a little feeling behind it."

"It's more than purely physical for me too, although, I have nothing against that either."

Susan laughed. "You are an honest man, Tanner; I'll say that for you."

Susan had breakfast on the table when Tanner asked about Amy.

"Oh, she spent the night at her boyfriend's place. I think I'll be losing a guest soon, because that boy is going to pop the question any day now if I had to guess."

"I'll spend the day with you at the restaurant, but tonight, Sammy and I have to go out again."

Susan sat down her coffee cup and looked at both of them. "Will it be dangerous?"

"Only for Calabrese," Tanner said.

Susan's phone rang. When she looked at the caller ID, she saw it was Amy calling. She was smiling when she answered the phone, but as she listened, she became solemn, and tears formed in her eyes.

"Oh God, Amy, I feel so bad for her. Yes honey, I'll see you later."

When the call ended, Susan pushed her plate away and wiped at her tears.

"What's wrong, Susan?" Tanner asked.

"A friend of mine, her son, Tyrone… he died last night after taking meth."

"Did he overdose?" Sammy asked.

"Amy said that the doctors think he had an undiagnosed heart condition, but if he hadn't taken the meth, it may have never bothered him." Susan stood. "I've got to give Maggie a call. That's Tyrone's mother. Tanner,

Tyrone was only sixteen, and I used to babysit him when he was a toddler. Oh God, what a waste, what a waste."

Susan drifted out of the room and Tanner saw that Sammy had grown angry.

"I know we just came down here to kill Volks, but maybe we can destroy his drug pipeline too."

"Yeah, but someone else will take Volks' place a week later."

"I know, and this is why my grandfather passed on the meth trade. He was all about giving people what they wanted, legal or not, but not that shit."

"Your grandfather wasn't good, but he was a good man."

"How well did you know him, Tanner?"

"Not well, but it's because of him that Joe and I are… close."

"How so?"

"He sent us out on a job once when we were about your age, and we got to know each other."

"This job, did you get it done?"

Tanner broke eye contact and looked off into space. "Yeah, we did what your grandfather asked. That's when I knew that Joe wasn't just another hood, and that he had a sense of honor."

"Who died?" Sammy asked.

Tanner sighed. "A very bad man."

"Good, then the world was better off without him."

Sammy went back to eating, but like Susan, Tanner found that his appetite had fled.

## 35
## SOULLESS JOE

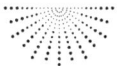

WILMINGTON, DELAWARE, ELEVEN YEARS EARLIER

THEY WATCHED CONTI ALL THAT DAY, WAITING TO SEE IF he'd run, but the good reverend only traveled between the shelter and the soup kitchen, and appeared to be going about his regular duties.

Tanner and Pullo also kept an eye out for any more retaliation because of what they'd done at the brothel, but it looked like no more trouble was coming from that direction.

Tanner had assumed that there wouldn't be. The madam would have been reluctant to admit to the people above her that two unarmed men had taken over her house.

He and Pullo had stolen no money. That meant she didn't have to come clean. Still, the men working for her wanted payback, so they had to go.

And despite the hookers having seen their faces, the

madam and her bodyguards were the only ones who could tie them to Conti. Now that they were gone, no one would know where to look for them.

Tanner saw that Pullo was becoming increasingly agitated as the day went on and Conti didn't budge. When Conti emerged late in the evening and headed for home, they fell in beside him.

"Like I said earlier, guys, do it at my apartment, that way the kids won't see."

"We're just walking with you for now," Pullo said.

Conti chuckled. "At least the shelter will be all right. I always knew that men like you would find me someday, and I took out a life insurance policy. After they find me, the shelter will have enough to keep running."

"Shut up," Pullo said. "I'm tired of hearing about how good you are now. You're still Carlo Conti and Carlo Conti is a scumbag."

"We're all sinners," Conti said.

CONTI'S APARTMENT WAS ON THE THIRD FLOOR OF AN OLD house that had started its existence as a single-family home, but which had been converted into ten separate dwellings. Tanner and Pullo followed Conti up a set of exterior back steps and into the tiny space.

It was one room with a bathroom the size of a closet, and other than a radio and a hot plate, Conti had few possessions.

"Monks live better than this," Pullo said.

Conti shrugged. "I eat most of my meals at the soup kitchen, and TV is nothing but crap."

Pullo looked at Tanner. "What the hell should I do here?"

"It's your move, Joe. I'm backup, remember?"

Pullo paced for a few seconds, then spun and pointed at Conti, who was seated on a ratty couch.

"I'm going to spend the night thinking things over, but one of us will be watching at all times. If you try to run, we'll make it hurt bad before we put you down."

Conti shrugged again. "You'll do what you have to do. I know your type and you lost your soul a long time ago. This delay is just your way of easing what's left of your conscience."

Pullo grunted and headed for the door.

"I'll leave that door unlocked for you," Conti called out.

When they reached the bottom of the stairs, Tanner asked Pullo if he wanted him to take the first watch.

"We're not watching him. I just said that. You saw him, he won't run. The bastard is almost looking forward to it."

"Why are you so angry?"

"Because this was supposed to be simple, Tanner. We were to find Carlo Conti and kill him. Now, instead of Conti, we've found a damn saint. C'mon, I'm going back to the motel to think."

They were two blocks from the motel when Tanner shouted for Pullo to pull the car to the curb.

When they were parked, Tanner opened his door.

"I think I saw someone lying back there in the bushes."

Pullo followed, and soon they were standing over the kid they had seen coming out of the motel room with

Hellman. The boy was badly beaten and barely conscious. When he moved, he grabbed his ribs, as if they were broken.

Tanner bent down and spoke to him. "Hey kid, who did this to you?"

"Some guy I don't know, but I think he was paid by Mr. Hellman. Hellman got real pissed when I asked him about Candy."

Pullo ran toward the pay phone on the corner. "I'll call for an ambulance."

"Who's Candy?"

"She's a friend, and a black hooker," the kid said, but the words were slurred, and it appeared painful to talk.

"This girl Candy went missing?"

"Yeah, I can't find her anywhere."

Pullo came back, and he and Tanner waited until they heard the ambulance approaching.

"Help is coming, kid, but we've got to go," Tanner said.

"Wait, there's one more thing."

Tanner bent down to listen, and what he heard gave him a very bad feeling.

36

# MONEY OR LOVE?

Merle and Earl sat on a porch swing together as they each stared down at one of the cards Mr. Wilson had left them.

"This is a whole mess of money, Merle."

"That it is, even after we give Hanna and Savannah their share, it'd still be a lot."

"And farmin' is hard work."

"Yep."

"If we did sell, do you think the girls would come back with us to New York?"

"No. You heard them last night. They don't like it there."

"Yeah, but I don't wanna lose Savannah. She's pretty as can be, and she likes me. When's the last time that happened?"

Merle gave it some thought. "Back in third grade, the Harper twins, Sissy Harper liked you."

"I don't want Sissy Harper. I want Savannah."

"I want Hanna."

The boys looked at each other and tossed the cards away.

INSIDE THE HOUSE, HANNA AND SAVANNAH SAT AT THE kitchen table and talked about the offer.

"You think they'll take it?" Savannah asked.

"That's a lot of money, and it's sure nice of them to pay us back for what we lost."

"We'd still never find a place like this again."

"No."

"If they sell, do you think they'll go back to New York?"

"Probably, and that Rossetti they worked for, he owned a titty bar, and you can just bet that those two had women crawlin' all over them night and day."

"I don't care what Earl used to do. He's nice to me and I'm fallin' for him."

"If they go back to New York we could go with them."

"I don't wanna live in New York, Hanna."

"Yeah, but you might have to if you wanna keep Earl."

Savannah picked up one of Mr. Wilson's cards and tore it in half.

"Stupid shoppin' center, and I miss the swamp too."

IN TENNESSEE, SAMMY WAS FOLLOWING GARRETT BATES' van while driving Tanner's rental. If Tanner's hunch was right, the newspaperman was involved with Volks.

Sammy followed Bates to a small warehouse just outside Brentwood, which housed a commercial printer.

He couldn't get close enough to see what was going on

without being spotted, but he assumed that Bates was picking up the newest addition of his weekly newspaper.

From there, Bates drove to another warehouse in a less affluent area, where two men dressed like bikers opened a gate and let him drive inside the parking lot.

Sammy smiled. It looked like Tanner was right. If so, they would soon have Volks where they wanted him.

## 37
## PAPER, MISTER?

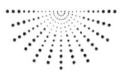

Tanner suggested to Susan that she and Amy go to the movies, just in case any of Calabrese's bikers decided to pay the house a visit while he and Sammy were gone.

Amy agreed to meet Susan in town later, and with Sammy out following Bates around, that left Tanner and Susan alone.

They ate dinner and then made love, and as Susan lay facing him, she asked questions.

"You're not the law, are you?"

"No."

"You're here to kill Calabrese?"

"Yes."

"What's his real name?"

"You're better off not knowing, but the reason I'm here is personal. He killed Sammy's father years ago when Sammy was just a boy."

"Oh, that is personal."

"I think this will all end tonight, and that means I'll be leaving tomorrow."

"Take me with you," Susan said, and then she laughed

and pointed at Tanner. "Oh, you should have seen your face. I was joking, Tanner. I'm not some lovesick schoolgirl, but you have left me with some good memories."

Tanner guided her onto her back. "Why don't we make one more?"

Susan giggled. "Good Lord but you recover quickly."

"It's all the clean living I do," Tanner said.

TANNER FOLLOWED SUSAN INTO TOWN WHILE RIDING Sammy's motorcycle. After watching her meet Amy in front of the movie theater, he rode three blocks south and met up with Sammy.

"He's still in there, Tanner, and he's alone as far as I can tell."

"Let's do this."

They left their vehicles, walked across the street, and down a driveway that ran alongside the newspaper office.

There was a wooden door at the rear of the building with a roll-up metal door at its left, and when Tanner tried them, he found that they both were locked.

He looked over at Sammy. "Did you bring what I told you to bring?"

"Yeah, I bought it while Bates was stopped for lunch."

Sammy reached behind his back and came out with a small crowbar.

"Once I pop this door, he might go for a weapon, so be ready."

Sammy nodded, and this time he took out a gun.

Tanner looked about to see if anyone was watching, but there was fencing separating the building from the one behind it, while the bakery to its left and the bank to its right had both closed for the day and had empty parking lots.

Tanner jammed the tip of the crowbar between the door and its frame, just above the lock. After wedging it in as far as he could, he began working it back and forth slowly, which gave him more room to jam it deeper inside, and with a violent jerk, the door popped open. It had made less noise than Tanner would have guessed, but it was still enough to alert Bates.

The newspaperman had been in the back of his panel van. When he peeked his bald head out of the rear, he saw Tanner walking toward him with a gun.

"Don't shoot me, Myers! I'm not armed."

Sammy looked inside the van and saw dozens of plastic bags containing white crystalline powder. There were also stacks of newspapers, and an old cigar box full of red rubber bands.

On the left side of the van were several rolled-up newspapers. When Tanner freed one from its rubber band, a baggie fell out.

Bates had been sitting on the floor of the van as he worked at concealing the baggies inside the newspapers, but he had gotten on his hands and knees to look out the back.

He was shaking violently, and his eyes never left Tanner's gun.

"Are you going to kill me?"

Tanner answered the man by slamming the gun across the side of his head and stunning him. He then held out his left hand, and Sammy handed him several zip ties.

Minutes later, Bates was bound up in the rear of the van with Tanner driving, as Sammy followed behind on the motorcycle.

38

## THE DANCE OF JOY

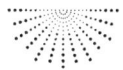

Merle and Earl had dinner with the girls, but none of them seemed very hungry.

After playing cards for a while, they went out and sat on the porch swings, but Earl sat with Merle, while Savannah settled beside her sister.

"Merle?"

"Yeah, Hanna?"

"When you sell the farm, Savannah and I wanna go to New York with you."

"You do?"

"Yeah, I mean, if you want us to come along."

Earl leaned forward and looked past his brother. "I guess you'd rather have the money than the farm, hmm?"

Savannah leaned forward too, as she looked past Hanna. "I don't want the damn money. I wanna be with you, dope."

Earl smiled and stood up. "Well, what about the farm?"

"I love the farm, but if you're goin' back to New York, well then, I'll go with you."

Hanna walked over and sat beside Merle.

"Would you stay here? I know it ain't New York City and that I'm not some fancy stripper, but I think we could do all right together, don't you?"

Merle smiled at Hanna while speaking to Earl. "We're stayin' little brother; the Carter boys are back home to stay."

Earl let out a whoop of joy, and Savannah flew into his arms.

IN NEW YORK, PULLO WAS AT LAUREL'S TOWNHOUSE AND playing cards with three of his men: Mike, Bosco, and Big Ralphie. He suspected they were letting him win.

It didn't surprise him. He remembered doing the same with Sam Giacconi. It took the thrill out of the game, so he folded his cards.

When the phone rang, Pullo wondered who was calling, but he didn't think much of it, and Laurel answered the call in the kitchen.

When she appeared in the doorway a few minutes later, he could tell that something had saddened her.

"What's up, baby?"

"That was Merle and Earl. They've decided to stay in Arkansas, but they said they would be back for the wedding."

"I guess they were homesick."

"Yes, but I'll still miss them, and I also want to meet these two women they keep talking about."

As Laurel went upstairs, Pullo contained his glee at the news until he was certain she was out of sight, and then he let it out.

Big Ralphie looked at Pullo in amazement. "Wow, boss. I've known you for years and that's the first time I've ever seen you dance."

39

# HUNTING AT NIGHT

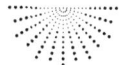

Tanner pulled the van to a stop on the side of a dirt road, before climbing into the rear of the vehicle, where he knelt beside Garrett Bates.

When Sammy pulled up on the bike, Tanner switched the dome light off before leaning over and opening the rear doors.

Bates was looking up at Tanner with eyes white with fear, and a sheen of sweat coated the man's bald head.

"Where and when do you meet Calabrese?"

"What?"

"He must talk to you in person sometime."

"Oh, yeah, there's a farm, an old deserted farm out on County Road West, but he doesn't come alone."

"How many guys does he have with him?"

"Two, and they're all armed. But listen, Myers, I'm cooperating, right? There's no reason to kill me."

Tanner whipped out a knife and cut Bates' hands free. "You're driving us to this farm."

"How did you know I was involved? Everyone thinks I hate Calabrese."

"Yeah, and you're still breathing, which made me wonder why he would put up with you and your newspaper. The cops would also never check your van because they trust you."

"The two guys coming with Volks, I bet they'll be the same two from the bar last night," Sammy said.

"Who's Volks?" Bates said.

"Never mind," Tanner said. "Just take us to this farm, and when we get there, you'll call Calabrese."

"Are you going to kill me?"

"Not if you do as I say."

"How can I trust you?"

"Bates, in about three seconds I'm going to smash you in the face if you don't stop talking; you can trust that."

Bates shut his mouth and Tanner freed his ankles from the zip ties.

CALABRESE SHOWED TWO HOURS LATER, AND AS SAMMY thought he would, he had the same two bruisers from the night before with him.

Bates was leaning back against the van casually. The rear doors were open a crack, and Sammy lay flat on his stomach with a gun pressed against the base of Bates' spine.

As they rode toward Bates, Calabrese and his men passed an old rusted Ford pickup on their left, which was sitting up on cinder blocks.

As the bikes rumbled by, Tanner sat up and then jumped out of the truck bed. He was running at full speed to catch up to the motorcycles, which began to slow as they neared the van.

One of the men must have caught sight of him in his mirror, because the bike swerved and then made to turn around. Tanner stopped running, dropped to one knee, and took aim at the dark shape of the rider's helmet, with help from the gun's laser sight.

The man was fumbling for a weapon beneath his jacket when the faceplate on the helmet shattered, and Tanner watched as the bike toppled over onto its side.

Knowing he'd been set up, Calabrese fired at the van and struck Bates twice in the chest, then revved up his bike to flee. Sammy exploded from the rear of the van and rolled to the ground. While lying on his stomach, he released several shots at Calabrese.

The shots missed Calabrese, but one of them wounded his other man. The man was hit in the back, and it caused him to swerve. When his front tire hit the rear of Calabrese's bike, both men lost control and went tumbling, as their motorcycles skidded off into the weeds bordering the surrounding forest.

Sammy was ahead of Tanner's position. He made it to his feet and went after Calabrese. He was so intent on catching the man that he ignored the biker he had wounded and ran right past him.

The biker pulled himself up to one elbow and took aim at Sammy with a long-barreled revolver. Before the man could pull the trigger, Tanner shot him in the back twice.

"Sammy! Slow down!"

There was no answer.

They had talked about this while waiting for Calabrese to show. Tanner had warned Sammy about the dangers of running into the woods at night, telling him that Calabrese could easily lay in wait or circle back.

The light was bad as well, for although there was

moonlight, clouds filled the sky and could render the forest pitch black without notice.

Tanner cursed, grabbed the dead man's fallen revolver, and ran into the shadows of the trees.

40

## PERSONAL BUSINESS

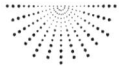

Sammy knew he was being stupid, but he couldn't imagine letting Volks just slip away.

He had been fourteen when Volks killed his father, Joseph Giacconi, and he still remembered the anguished look on his grandfather's face when he told him of his father's death.

From that day on, his grandfather tried to protect him and keep him out of the life, but he knew where he belonged even while he was in college in California. It was the main reason he had returned to New York City to live.

Sophia's face flashed across his consciousness and he smiled.

She had been a surprise.

He hadn't been in love since he had a crush on a girl in high school and figured he would never fall that hard again. But after one look at Sophia Verona, he knew he couldn't forget her.

"I have to make it back to her," he whispered to himself, and a second later, he heard the crunch of leaves to his right.

Sammy dropped and rolled behind a tree as three rounds passed through the space where his chest had been an instant before.

~

Tanner saw the muzzle flashes coming from up ahead and to his left. When there was no accompanying cry of pain, he knew the shots either had been fatal or had missed. What he didn't know was who had fired them, but suspected it was Calabrese given the gun's sound. He hoped Sammy had the presence of mind to turn off the laser sight on his weapon.

Tanner moved as soundlessly as possible through the trees and heard someone approaching. Calabrese, who was Bobby Volks, was tall and outweighed Sammy by a good fifty pounds. Tanner waited for whoever was coming to get closer. If he could see their silhouette, he'd know who it was.

When the lumbering shape came toward him, he knew it was Volks. He raised his gun to fire, but then thought of Sammy.

The kid needed to put Volks down.

Tanner hid behind a tree and waited.

Volks appeared seconds later holding a gun in his right hand while he fumbled with a phone in his left. He was about to call in reinforcements, but he'd never get the chance.

As Volks passed him, Tanner smashed the revolver he'd taken off the dead man against the back of Volks' head.

The big man tumbled to the ground and Tanner rushed over and snatched his weapon away, before crushing the phone with the heel of his boot.

Volks looked up at him with dazed eyes, but had stayed conscious, as Tanner hoped he would.

Sounds came from behind them and Tanner realized that Sammy was growing nearer. He emptied the remaining rounds from Volks' gun into his hand, just as the man stood up on unsteady legs.

Tanner sat on the ground and tossed the empty gun back to Volks.

"Catch."

Volks, still dazed, nearly dropped the weapon, but he managed not to lose it. He was holding it in his right hand when Sammy came into view.

"Volks!"

Hearing Sammy call him by his old name shocked Calabrese to full alertness, and he tensed up.

Sammy fired twice, both shots hitting Volks, one in his right shoulder, while the other hit him in the side. Volks dropped to his knees as the gun fell from his hand, and Sammy walked over and placed his weapon against Volks' forehead.

"Tanner, were you hit?"

"No, but you've got good timing. He was just about to shoot me."

Sammy pressed the gun hard against Volks. "Bohdan Volkov, my name is Sammy Giacconi, Joe Giacconi's son."

Volks seemed to shrink in on himself. "We were at war, kid. It wasn't personal."

"This is," Sammy said, and he pulled the trigger.

The rear of Volks' head exploded in a spray of gore as the body tumbled backwards.

Sammy stood there staring down at Volks, as his face wore a look of satisfaction.

"That was for you, Dad."

A moment passed before Sammy turned away from the

body. Tanner gave the corpse a final look, then followed Sammy back to the farm.

They found Bates a dozen yards away from the van. He was dead; he had bled out from his wounds.

Sammy tossed his chin toward the interior of the van. "What should we do with the meth?"

"Leave it. I'll make an anonymous call to the cops."

After righting one of the fallen bikes, Tanner got it started, but as he straddled it, Sammy motioned for him to cut the engine.

"Thank you, Tanner. I know that being around me was the last thing you wanted to do, because of Sophia and all, but I couldn't have done this without you."

"You did good, Sammy, and I know that Joe will be proud of you. As far as Sophia, just take care of her, okay?"

"I love her, Tanner."

Sammy climbed aboard his bike, and Bobby Volks became part of the past.

## 41
## DEATH AND DECEIT

WILMINGTON, DELAWARE, ELEVEN YEARS EARLIER

At 4:19 a.m., Tanner and Pullo climbed the back stairs to Carlo Conti's apartment.

As Tanner stayed back, Pullo tried the doorknob, and as Conti had said it would be, it was unlocked.

Pullo flicked his head around the doorframe and saw Conti sitting on his tattered sofa. He was dressed as he had been the day before and looked as if he had been awake all night. In his lap was an open bible. Pullo motioned for Tanner to follow, and then he approached Conti.

Conti smiled up at him grimly. "I see you're a good soldier."

Pullo looked unnerved by the words, but he did what he came there to do.

They returned to New York City before noon and were seated in front of Sam Giacconi's desk.

"If you're back, that means you've found him," Giacconi said.

"Yeah, we found him, Sam," Pullo said. "We found Conti. The bastard is dead."

"Good work, and Tanner here backed you up?"

"Yeah, Tanner is all right, and I'd use him again."

"Great. Now Joey, go see your mom, she called here looking for you."

Pullo stood, and Tanner rose with him.

Sam Giacconi reached across the desk and shook Tanner's hand. "Thanks for helping my boy."

"Anytime," Tanner said.

The two of them left the funeral home and walked down the alley in the rear, where a hearse was parked. Across the street, a bell rang at a red brick factory and workers streamed from the building for their lunch break.

As a white Hummer drove by, Pullo followed the mammoth vehicle with his eyes, and there was a look of envy toward the driver.

"I'm going to get one of those someday."

"You okay, Joe?"

"Yeah, Tanner, in the end we all do what we have to do… still, I hated lying to Sam."

The kid who had been beaten told Tanner and Pullo about the missing black prostitute named Candy, but before they left him, he told them that Candy had two daughters.

Pullo hadn't wanted to believe in Tanner's theory, while thinking about it made him want to vomit.

"Child welfare must have them."

"Maybe, but I've got to know one way or another."

Pullo stared at him for long seconds and then nodded. "I'm with you."

"We'll go in around four, that's when the guard at the door will be at his lowest point."

"Yeah, but what if more guys show?"

"Then we go in sooner."

"How do you want to do this?"

Tanner smiled. "I have a plan."

At 3:58 a.m., Pullo staggered out of his motel room with a bottle in his hand, while mumbling to himself.

He immediately caught the attention of the man across the courtyard who was guarding Room 16. The man was white, tall, and lanky, and there was the bulge of a shoulder holster beneath his jacket. The guard sat up straighter in his chair as he cleared his throat. Pullo wondered if he might have been asleep.

Pullo walked toward him while still staggering, coming at the man from his right.

"Go back in your room and sleep it off, dude," the guard said.

Pullo ignored him and drew closer.

The man had just taken his gun out to threaten Pullo when Tanner came up behind the guard and jammed an ice pick into the back of his neck.

The man fell to the walkway while twitching in his death throes, and Pullo caught the gun before it could hit the ground. Tanner found the keys for the lock in the man's jacket pocket and opened the door.

Pullo crossed himself for the first time in years as his

eyes fell on the daughters of the prostitute named Candy. The two girls were six and seven years old. Hellman had been pimping them out to pedophiles for nearly a week after murdering their mother and disposing of her body.

CONTI WAS WAITING FOR PULLO TO TAKE OUT A GUN AND shoot him when he spotted Tanner walking through the doorway. Tanner was carrying the two girls, whom he and Pullo had rescued after wrapping them in blankets.

Hellman had kept the children naked and chained to a bed.

Conti stood. "What is this?"

Pullo explained quickly, and Conti looked as sickened by the tale as Pullo felt.

"You'll take care of them?" Tanner asked.

"Of course, but I don't have a phone. Please call an ambulance for these children. They need to see a doctor."

The two black girls sat on Conti's couch in a near-catatonic state, and Tanner wondered if either of them would ever lead a normal life.

Pullo placed a hand on Conti's shoulder. "We were never here, and as far as we're concerned, Carlo Conti is dead."

"Thank you. And please, make that call. These children need help."

Tanner sent Conti a nod, took one last look at the girls, and left to call the ambulance.

HELLMAN ARRIVED AT THE MOTEL JUST AFTER SEVEN A.M. When he saw that the bodyguard wasn't at his post, he went to investigate. That's when he noticed that the door to Room 16 was sitting ajar.

As he stepped into the room, Hellman spotted the money that had been flung across the bed. It drew him in, as Tanner knew it would.

However, when he saw the feet of the bodyguard sticking out of the bathroom, Hellman inhaled sharply and peddled backwards.

That's when Tanner and Pullo entered and slammed the door shut.

Hellman spun around and tried the fake smile. "Those girls earn a fortune; I'll cut you both in."

Tanner and Pullo raised their weapons simultaneously and emptied them into Hellman.

They were in the car and out on the highway in seconds, headed back to New York City, while bonded by death and deceit.

"You didn't lie to Giacconi. You told him we found Conti, and you told him that a bastard was dead, both of those things are true."

Pullo shook his head. "I still lied, but I can live with it."

"I'll see you around, Joe."

"Yeah, Tanner, keep in touch."

The two men separated, not as friends, but no longer strangers.

42

MAN OF MYSTERY

Tanner found Susan wide awake and dressed in a robe. She was seated on her porch awaiting his return.

After a kiss of greeting, she looked at him questioningly, and he answered her with only two words.

"It's done."

Susan then reached out, took Sammy's hand, and gave it a squeeze. "How do you feel?"

Sammy looked startled by the question, and Susan's empathy, but after letting out a sigh, he answered her.

"Better, I feel better."

"Amy volunteered to cook breakfast tomorrow because it's her day off, so she'll be up early."

"I wouldn't count on her having the day off," Tanner said.

Susan understood his meaning, and the three of them went inside.

Tanner explained to Susan what had happened without going into detail. When he told her about Garrett Bates, she seemed surprised.

"He's a—he was a town hero and was going to run for mayor next year. He was also Tyrone's Boy Scout Troop Leader. He helped to bring that poison into the county? It makes you wonder about everyone."

"It was likely greed that drove him, and I'm sure he was paid well."

"Did you kill him?"

"No. Calabrese killed him."

"I never liked Garrett, that way, but I did like him as a friend, and I admired him too."

"Then I'm sorry you lost your friend."

"Don't be, and enough talk, it's late and I want to go to bed."

Tanner held her as they lay in bed facing each other.

"I'm going to miss you," Susan said. "But right now, I'm too damn tired to show you how much."

"You can show me in the morning."

Susan snuggled closer. "You remind me of my husband. He was a man of action too. Even when he was home on leave, I could tell that he wanted to get back into battle."

"And it left you a young widow."

"Yes, but I wouldn't trade my years with him for anything. Is that why you've never married? Are you afraid to leave behind a widow?"

"There is one woman I would have married, and now she's marrying someone else."

"You let her get away."

"No. I ran from her. I didn't like the way she made me feel."

Susan sat up on one elbow and stared at Tanner. "You

were afraid of her because you were beginning to depend on her."

Tanner ran his hand over his face. "This is what I get for sleeping with a woman as wise as you. You read me too well. I also talk too much around you."

Susan snuggled against him again. "Yes, and it's because I'm safe. After tomorrow, we'll probably never see each other again, and truthfully, I don't even know who you are."

"You know more than most," Tanner said, then the two of them drifted off to sleep.

THE NEXT DAY, TANNER SAID GOODBYE TO SUSAN AS THEY stood by his rental.

Sammy had left early, after saying that there was something he wanted to do, and as Tanner had predicted, Amy was called in to help with the mess out at the abandoned farm.

Susan cupped Tanner's face in her hands and kissed him one last time.

"Goodbye man of mystery, and you be careful."

"I will, and who knows, maybe we'll meet again someday."

"Maybe," Susan said, although they both knew how unlikely it was.

Tanner climbed in the car, said goodbye, and headed to the airport.

Susan had eased his ache at having lost Sophia, but as he drove along, he found himself longing for more time with both of them. That brought thoughts of several other women he'd known over the years, including Laurel.

When the melancholy threatened to swallow him, he

did what he always did. He pushed it behind him into the past where it belonged.

The world was full of women such as Susan, Sophia, and Laurel.

At least, that's what he told himself.

43

SAM THE MAN

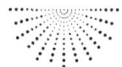

After Tanner returned his rental, he was beginning to wonder if Sammy was going to miss the flight. That's when he spotted him walking toward him.

Sammy had changed his look. The long hair was gone, and Tanner could see the man's resemblance to his late grandfather and namesake more clearly.

Sammy was also dressed in a dark suit, but like Tanner, he wore no tie. He walked up to Tanner with a small smile playing at his lips.

"What do you think?"

"I don't think anyone will call you kid anymore," Tanner said.

"Yeah, it was time I grew up a little."

After they had passed through security, Sammy asked Tanner what he had done with the weapons they used.

"I disassembled them, and then I tossed the pieces in a lake on my way to the airport."

"I would've liked to have kept that gun as a souvenir, but I don't think the airline would have appreciated me bringing it onboard the plane."

"Yeah, they're funny that way," Tanner said.

A short time later, they were in the air, as Sammy headed back to Sophia, and Tanner simply headed back.

## 44

## CHAOS

Pullo was smiling wide.

He had learned that Sammy had killed Bobby Volks. Pullo was leaving to meet with Tanner at The Americana Sports Bar to get details about the hit.

He walked into the kitchen and found Laurel sipping on a cup of coffee while looking through a bridal magazine, as Big Ralphie sat to her left, eating a pizza.

"I won't be long, baby, but please stay inside while I'm gone."

Laurel stood and kissed him. "Is it really necessary for me to stay home? I'd be just as safe at the clinic."

"I don't want to take a chance, and Big Ralphie will keep you safe."

Big Ralphie had a mouthful of pizza, but he sent Pullo a thumbs-up sign.

Pullo was leaving Laurel's townhouse when one of his men, Mike, pointed toward two figures getting out of a car. Mike was a big man around forty, with wide shoulders.

Pullo looked where Mike was pointing and saw Tamir Ivanov and Justina Moretti walking toward him. The two were smiling at each other while talking quietly.

"Those two are Feds, right, boss?"

"Yeah, they're Feds, Mike."

The other man with Pullo was named Bosco. He was as big as Mike, but younger, and he watched Justina intently as she walked toward them.

"Fed or not, that chick is hot."

"That she is," Pullo said.

Mike and Bosco were two of three bodyguards. Bosco and Mike were always with Pullo, while Big Ralphie stayed near Laurel at all times.

Inside the townhouse, Big Ralphie spoke to Laurel between inhaling slices of pizza.

"You want a large wedding, don't you?"

Laurel nodded shyly. "I do, and I know it's silly since I was married once before, but it is something I've always dreamed of having."

"Tell the boss. He's crazy about you. I'm sure he'd spring for it."

"I know he would. But he has a lot on his mind, and a large wedding would be a distraction he doesn't need. A small wedding will do fine."

"Doc Ivy, I've got five younger sisters and a ton of female cousins, so I know what girls are like. Talk to the boss. Joe will make it happen, and then you won't always wish you had done it."

Laurel grinned. "I'll think about it." The grin disappeared as she remembered something and stood up. "I forgot to ask Joe to stop by the clinic and grab my laptop."

Laurel hurried to catch up to Pullo, and Big Ralphie raised a hand to tell her to wait for him. Laurel didn't notice, and with his mouth full of pizza, Big Ralphie couldn't call out.

"We need to talk, Pullo," Ivanov said.

"What's this about?" Pullo said.

"It's about your life," Justina said. "The DEA caught wind of an assassination plot against you, and we're not talking Krupin here. These are people that know what they're doing."

"We'll talk inside," Pullo said.

"No, not inside," Ivanov said. "We need to get you someplace safe."

Pullo was about to ask him what he meant, when the door opened, and Laurel looked out at the gathering.

"What's going on, Joe?"

"It's okay, honey; they're just here to talk."

Justina headed up the stairs. "Miss Ivy? I'm Agent Moretti of the FBI, please come with us, ma'am. We don't believe it's safe to be—"

Justina never finished her sentence, as a bullet struck her in the side and ruptured her heart. It was the first shot fired by one of the four men who had just emerged from the underground parking garage on the opposite side of the street.

"Justina!" Ivanov cried out to his partner, and then watched as she tumbled down the stairs backwards as limp as a rag doll. She landed at his feet face up, and he knew by her lifeless eyes that she was gone.

Two cars had been approaching the nearby intersection. The lead driver slammed on his brakes, causing a collision. Then, the drivers of both vehicles abandoned them and ran for cover, joining the pedestrians who had already done the same while screaming in panic.

The first bullet was followed by dozens, and as Pullo moved toward the stairs to get to Laurel, Mike tackled him to the ground.

"Down, boss!"

Pullo hit the ground hard, looked up, and saw several bullets break windows and chip at the stone surrounding Laurel, who had frozen in place from fear.

Then Big Ralphie was there. He grabbed Laurel around the waist and turned with her, using his massive body to shield her, and as he did so, he was struck three times. Still, he managed to shove Laurel back inside the townhouse before collapsing in the doorway.

"Get off me!" Pullo shouted, as he pushed Mike aside. Only then did he see the fatal wound. Mike had been struck in the right temple by a ricochet off the stone steps. At the back of his head was a large exit wound.

Pullo looked around and saw that Bosco was wounded in the left arm, but still able to fight, while Ivanov was on his knees and crying over his partner's body. The only thing that had saved the federal agent was the fact that he was aligned with the Hummer's rear wheel well, and the shots couldn't penetrate the steel.

Pullo lunged over, pushed Ivanov to the ground, then slapped him hard across the face.

"Help me kill these bastards!"

Ivanov grunted and took out his gun, as tears still fell from his eyes.

The barrage of shots seemed unending because the shooters were pros. While two of them fired, the other two reloaded, and there seemed no end to their ammo.

Pullo left the cover of the Hummer's wheel well and crawled beneath the vehicle. It was a tight fit, as two of the tires were flat.

He could see the men, and what looked like a thousand shell casings were sprinkled at their feet. Pullo took aim at those feet and fired, just as Ivanov crawled up beside him.

The first man fell to his knees as Ivanov shot a second man in the shin. The third man realized what was happening, turned, and ran, while the fourth man dropped flat while firing.

It did him no good, as Pullo and Ivanov had kept up a barrage of their own, and they killed the three men where they fell.

Meanwhile, Bosco fired at the man who had fled and struck him in the right calf muscle, causing the man to stumble and fall.

After crawling out from under the car, Pullo was horrified to see Laurel return outside. He ran to her and met her on the steps.

"It's not safe yet; get back in."

"Are you all right, Joe?"

"I'm good, baby, and thank God for Big Ralphie."

Laurel turned and stared at Big Ralphie. "Oh my God."

Pullo had thought Big Ralphie dead, but the huge man was simply unconscious, and had just rolled onto his side. His face looked as purple as a plum.

"He can't breathe," Laurel said. "He was eating when this all started; I think he's choking on the food he had in his mouth."

Laurel slammed her hand hard against Big Ralphie's

back to try to dislodge the obstruction, and her palm came away wet with blood from his wounds. With the big man unconscious and lying on his side, the Heimlich maneuver was out, and Big Ralphie was running out of time.

"Joe, hand me your knife, and I'll also need a pen."

"Laurel, you're not safe out here."

"Joe, he saved me, and I can save him, but I need your knife."

Pullo passed her his knife as he looked around for new threats. There were none, but Ivanov and Bosco had the surviving shooter up and hopping along on one leg.

"I need that pen, or some kind of tube," Laurel said.

Pullo didn't have a pen, but Ivanov did, and he passed it over.

"A tracheotomy?" he asked Laurel.

"Yes," Laurel said, as she took the pen apart. She then felt along Big Ralphie's neck, near his Adam's apple, as she searched for the cricothyroid membrane. When she located it, she made a small incision with the knife, then another into the membrane beneath it. With that done, she carefully inserted the empty casing of Ivanov's pen, and then blew several short breaths into it.

When she felt air coming from the tube, she looked at Big Ralphie's chest and saw it moving. He was breathing on his own.

Laurel laughed with relief. "He's getting air."

Pullo smiled at her. "Good baby, but now go back inside."

With Big Ralphie breathing and the emergency ended, Laurel looked about at the carnage scattered around Pullo's Hummer, which had more holes than a cheese grater.

Justina lay on the sidewalk like a broken doll, where

mere moments earlier, she was speaking to Laurel. Three of the shooters, all stout and swarthy men, were lying in the street dead, each with multiple wounds, while Mike was also dead, and Bosco winced from the wound in his left arm.

Laurel stepped toward Bosco to offer aid, but Pullo took her by the shoulders.

"Baby, please go back inside. I'd die if anything happened to you."

"I should help Bosco."

Bosco sent her a smile. "I'm good, Doc, just take cover."

"See, he's good," Pullo said.

Laurel wiped away tears. "Come with me."

"I'll be right in, now please go."

Laurel pointed down at Big Ralphie. "That's a temporary measure, he needs an ER, and he's wounded besides."

"There's help coming, hear it?" Pullo said, and Laurel smiled when she listened and heard the sirens in the distance.

After Laurel went back inside, Pullo stared down at the surviving cartel hitman.

He spoke to the punk in Spanish and saw him sneer.

"Your Spanish sucks, Pullo."

"Good, you speak English."

"Yeah, I should, I grew up in El Paso. And don't think you've won. They'll send more guys, and you don't have Tanner to cover your ass anymore either."

"What's that mean?"

"It means he's dead, cabrón. Your boy is dead."

Pullo grabbed the punk by his collar and the man winced from the pain in his leg.

"You're lying!"

"Hey man, his ass got blown up in a house. Tanner is dead man, and you're next."

Pullo fell back against the wall just as two police cruisers came into view. They were followed by an ambulance, and there were more flashing lights in the distance.

"Tanner can't be dead, he—wait a second. What house are you talking about?"

"Out on Staten Island, where that slut of his lives."

Pullo reached up and grabbed the sides of his head with both hands. "Oh God, you're talking about Sammy and Sophia."

The man pointed down at Justina's body, as he had just noticed the badge on her belt. "Oh shit, that one was a cop? Good for the bitch!"

Ivanov grabbed the man by the hair and tossed him down the stone steps. There was a loud cracking noise when the punk landed. He screamed in pain and held his broken left kneecap.

Ivanov spat at the thug and then looked over at Pullo and Bosco.

"We didn't see shit," Pullo said. He took out his phone and began dialing, as Ivanov lofted his credentials in the air and went to talk to the arriving cops.

There was no answer, by either Sammy or Sophia.

"His cab got lost. He never made it to the house. It was somebody else," Pullo said, as he tried to convince himself of a lie.

WHEN IVANOV WAS ABLE TO CONFIRM THE PUNK'S STORY, Pullo learned the truth.

"It happened while we were being attacked, Pullo.

They're still putting out the fire, but they say the house is gone. It's why we wanted to move you. The cartel plays hardball."

"Tell me where Krupin is."

"You want to kill him?"

"You're goddamn right," Pullo said.

Ivanov looked over to where a pair of workers from the coroners' office were zipping Justina into a body bag.

"You're going to have to get in line, Pullo. Krupin is mine."

# 45
# STRANGE BEDFELLOWS

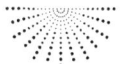

## MIDNIGHT ON STATEN ISLAND

Pullo told his men to stay back as he walked over to the pile of rubble that had been the home of Sophia Verona.

Tanner was there, and was standing before the thick web of red ARSON INVESTIGATION tape left by the fire department. He was staring at the debris with eyes of ice.

Pullo stood beside him.

"How is Sammy?" Tanner said.

"He's alive, which is a miracle, but he's still in a coma, and one leg is badly broken."

The fire department discovered Sammy's naked battered body lying beneath the bathtub. The explosion had blown it out of the house and into a neighbor's yard.

As near as they could tell with a preliminary investigation, the bomb had been left beneath the bed, a bed Sophia had been lying upon as she waited for Sammy to finish his bath.

Tanner turned and looked at Pullo. "You said on the phone that this was the work of a cartel. That means they won't stop coming."

"Yeah, Krupin went and got himself some heavy hitters."

"I'll need details, Joe, as many as you can get me. A list of the key players, what they look like, where they are, and I don't just mean here, but Mexico too."

"You can't kill them all, Tanner. There are too many."

Tanner shook his head. "No, not too many, just one, and then another, and another, and another. By the time I'm done with them, there will be none left."

A car pulled up and Pullo's men went on high alert. Bosco was one of them, with his wounded arm in a sling. When he saw that it was Ivanov, he gave the all clear.

"Who's that?" Tanner said.

"He's the Fed I told you about."

Ivanov walked over and stood beside Pullo, then, he looked past him.

"Are you Tanner?"

"Yes."

"Are you as good as they say you are?"

"No. I'm better."

Ivanov was still wearing a suit, and there was a white envelope sticking out of the breast pocket. He removed it, leaned past Pullo, and handed it to Tanner.

"What is this?" Tanner said.

"That's a copy of the latest intelligence we have, names, locations, and pictures. There are over thirty men there, and they're a mix of Russian mob and cartel members. We haven't located Krupin yet, but we will."

"I thought you weren't dirty, Ivanov?" Pullo said.

"I don't want your money, Pullo. I want blood for Justina."

"That was his partner," Pullo told Tanner, although he was beginning to suspect there had been more than that between them.

Tanner held up the envelope. "I'll put this to good use."

"I was never here," Ivanov said, and headed back to his car.

Pullo watched him leave. "Krupin pissed off the wrong Fed."

"Do you remember how we met, Joe?"

"You handed me Vincenzo Rigoletto's head in a box."

"This time, the head will be Krupin's."

Tanner walked to a car and drove off, to begin his reign of death.

TANNER RETURNS!

*BALLET OF DEATH - BOOK 9*

## AFTERWORD

Thank you,

REMINGTON KANE

## JOIN MY INNER CIRCLE

You'll receive FREE books, such as,

SLAY BELLS – A TANNER NOVEL – BOOK 0
TAKEN! ALPHABET SERIES – 26 ORIGINAL TAKEN! TALES

Also – Exclusive short stories featuring TANNER, along with other books.

TO BECOME AN INNER CIRCLE MEMBER, GO TO:
http://remingtonkane.com/mailing-list/

ALSO BY REMINGTON KANE

**The TANNER Series in order**

INEVITABLE I - A Tanner Novel - Book 1

KILL IN PLAIN SIGHT - A Tanner Novel - Book 2

MAKING A KILLING ON WALL STREET - A Tanner Novel - Book 3

THE FIRST ONE TO DIE LOSES - A Tanner Novel - Book 4

THE LIFE & DEATH OF CODY PARKER - A Tanner Novel - Book 5

WAR - A Tanner Novel- A Tanner Novel - Book 6

SUICIDE OR DEATH - A Tanner Novel - Book 7

TWO FOR THE KILL - A Tanner Novel - Book 8

BALLET OF DEATH - A Tanner Novel - Book 9

MORE DANGEROUS THAN MAN - A Tanner Novel - Book 10

TANNER TIMES TWO - A Tanner Novel - Book 11

OCCUPATION: DEATH - A Tanner Novel - Book 12

HELL FOR HIRE - A Tanner Novel - Book 13

A HOME TO DIE FOR - A Tanner Novel - Book 14

FIRE WITH FIRE - A Tanner Novel - Book 15

TO KILL A KILLER - A Tanner Novel - Book 16

WHITE HELL – A Tanner Novel - Book 17

MANHATTAN HIT MAN – A Tanner Novel - Book 18

ONE HUNDRED YEARS OF TANNER – A Tanner Novel -

Book 19

REVELATIONS - A Tanner Novel - Book 20

THE SPY GAME - A Tanner Novel - Book 21

A VICTIM OF CIRCUMSTANCE - A Tanner Novel - Book 22

A MAN OF RESPECT - A Tanner Novel - Book 23

THE MAN, THE MYTH - A Tanner Novel - Book 24

ALL-OUT WAR - A Tanner Novel - Book 25

THE REAL DEAL - A Tanner Novel - Book 26

WAR ZONE - A Tanner Novel - Book 27

ULTIMATE ASSASSIN - A Tanner Novel - Book 28

KNIGHT TIME - A Tanner Novel - Book 29

PROTECTOR - A Tanner Novel - Book 30

BULLETS BEFORE BREAKFAST - A Tanner Novel - Book 31

VENGEANCE - A Tanner Novel - Book 32

TARGET: TANNER - A Tanner Novel - Book 33

BLACK SHEEP - A Tanner Novel - Book 34

FLESH AND BLOOD - A Tanner Novel - Book 35

NEVER SEE IT COMING - A Tanner Novel - Book 36

MISSING - A Tanner Novel - Book 37

CONTENDER - A Tanner Novel - Book 38

TO SERVE AND PROTECT - A Tanner Novel - Book 39

STALKING HORSE - A Tanner Novel - Book 40

THE EVIL OF TWO LESSERS - A Tanner Novel - Book 41

SINS OF THE FATHER AND MOTHER - A Tanner Novel - Book 42

SOULLESS - A Tanner Novel - Book 43

**The Young Guns Series in order**

YOUNG GUNS

YOUNG GUNS 2 - SMOKE & MIRRORS

YOUNG GUNS 3 - BEYOND LIMITS

YOUNG GUNS 4 - RYKER'S RAIDERS

YOUNG GUNS 5 - ULTIMATE TRAINING

YOUNG GUNS 6 - CONTRACT TO KILL

YOUNG GUNS 7 - FIRST LOVE

YOUNG GUNS 8 - THE END OF THE BEGINNING

**A Tanner Series in order**

TANNER: YEAR ONE

TANNER: YEAR TWO

TANNER: YEAR THREE

TANNER: YEAR FOUR

TANNER: YEAR FIVE

**The TAKEN! Series in order**

TAKEN! - LOVE CONQUERS ALL - Book 1

TAKEN! - SECRETS & LIES - Book 2

TAKEN! - STALKER - Book 3

TAKEN! - BREAKOUT! - Book 4

TAKEN! - THE THIRTY-NINE - Book 5

TAKEN! - KIDNAPPING THE DEVIL - Book 6

TAKEN! - HIT SQUAD - Book 7

TAKEN! - MASQUERADE - Book 8

TAKEN! - SERIOUS BUSINESS - Book 9

TAKEN! - THE COUPLE THAT SLAYS TOGETHER - Book 10

TAKEN! - PUT ASUNDER - Book 11

TAKEN! - LIKE BOND, ONLY BETTER - Book 12

TAKEN! - MEDIEVAL - Book 13

TAKEN! - RISEN! - Book 14

TAKEN! - VACATION - Book 15

TAKEN! - MICHAEL - Book 16

TAKEN! - BEDEVILED - Book 17

TAKEN! - INTENTIONAL ACTS OF VIOLENCE - Book 18

TAKEN! - THE KING OF KILLERS – Book 19

TAKEN! - NO MORE MR. NICE GUY - Book 20 & the Series Finale

**The MR. WHITE Series**

PAST IMPERFECT - MR. WHITE - Book 1

HUNTED - MR. WHITE - Book 2

**The BLUE STEELE Series in order**

BLUE STEELE - BOUNTY HUNTER- Book 1

BLUE STEELE - BROKEN- Book 2

BLUE STEELE - VENGEANCE- Book 3

BLUE STEELE - THAT WHICH DOESN'T KILL ME- Book 4

BLUE STEELE - ON THE HUNT- Book 5

BLUE STEELE - PAST SINS - Book 6

BLUE STEELE - DADDY'S GIRL - Book 7 & the Series Finale

**The CALIBER DETECTIVE AGENCY Series in order**

CALIBER DETECTIVE AGENCY - GENERATIONS- Book 1

CALIBER DETECTIVE AGENCY - TEMPTATION- Book 2

CALIBER DETECTIVE AGENCY - A RANSOM PAID IN BLOOD- Book 3

CALIBER DETECTIVE AGENCY - MISSING- Book 4

CALIBER DETECTIVE AGENCY - DECEPTION- Book 5

CALIBER DETECTIVE AGENCY - CRUCIBLE- Book 6

CALIBER DETECTIVE AGENCY – LEGENDARY – Book 7

CALIBER DETECTIVE AGENCY – WE ARE GATHERED HERE TODAY - Book 8

CALIBER DETECTIVE AGENCY - MEANS, MOTIVE, and OPPORTUNITY - Book 9 & the Series Finale

**THE TAKEN!/TANNER Series in order**

THE CONTRACT: KILL JESSICA WHITE - Taken!/Tanner - Book 1

UNFINISHED BUSINESS – Taken!/Tanner – Book 2

THE ABDUCTION OF THOMAS LAWSON - Taken!/Tanner – Book 3

PREDATOR - Taken!/Tanner - Book 4

**DETECTIVE PIERCE Series in order**

MONSTERS - A Detective Pierce Novel - Book 1

DEMONS - A Detective Pierce Novel - Book 2

ANGELS - A Detective Pierce Novel - Book 3

**THE OCEAN BEACH ISLAND Series in order**

THE MANY AND THE ONE - Book 1
SINS & SECOND CHANES - Book 2
DRY ADULTERY, WET AMBITION -Book 3
OF TONGUE AND PEN - Book 4
ALL GOOD THINGS… - Book 5
LITTLE WHITE SINS - Book 6
THE LIGHT OF DARKNESS - Book 7
STERN ISLAND - Book 8 & the Series Finale

**THE REVENGE Series in order**

JOHNNY REVENGE - The Revenge Series - Book 1
THE APPOINTMENT KILLER - The Revenge Series - Book 2
AN I FOR AN I - The Revenge Series - Book 3

**ALSO**

THE EFFECT: Reality is changing!
THE FIX-IT MAN: A Tale of True Love and Revenge
DOUBLE OR NOTHING
PARKER & KNIGHT
REDEMPTION: Someone's taken her
DESOLATION LAKE
TIME TRAVEL TALES & OTHER SHORT STORIES

**TWO FOR THE KILL**
**Copyright © REMINGTON KANE, 2015**
**YEAR ZERO PUBLISHING**

This book is a work of fiction. Names, characters, places and incidents either are products of the author's imagination or are used fictitiously.

Any resemblance to actual events or locales or persons, living or dead, is entirely coincidental.

All rights reserved. Except as permitted under the U.S. Copyright Act of 1976, no part of this publication may be reproduced, distributed or transmitted in any form or by any means, or stored in a database or retrieval system, without the prior written permission of the publisher.

❦ Created with Vellum